Pleasure in Reading

FIRST CHOICE

selected by
MICHAEL MARLAND BA
Director of Studies, Crown Woods School, London

Illustrated by David Gormley

Longman

LONGMAN GROUP LIMITED
London

*Associated companies, branches and
representatives throughout the world*

This edition © Longman Group Ltd 1971

*First published 1971
Fifth impression 1975
ISBN 0 582 18659 5*

Acknowledgements

We are grateful to the following for permission to reproduce copyright material:

Jonathan Cape Limited for 'Mother and Son' from *The Short Stories of Liam O'Flaherty*; Jonathan Cape Limited and Charles Scribner's Sons for 'Ha'Penny' from *Debbie Go Home and Other Stories* and *Tales from a Troubled Land* by Alan Paton, copyright © 1961 Alan Paton; author and author's agents for 'The Shaft' from *The Leaping Lad* by Sid Chaplin; Chatto and Windus Limited for an extract from *Border Country* by Raymond Williams; George G. Harrap & Company Limited for 'Spit Nolan' from *The Goalkeeper's Revenge* by Bill Naughton; Michael Joseph Limited for 'One of the Virtues' from *The Desperadoes* by Stan Barstow; author and author's agents for 'Through the Tunnel' from *The Habit of Loving* by Doris Lessing; Macgibbon and Kee Limited for 'Taddy the Lamplighter' from *Late Night on Watling Street and Other Stories* by Bill Naughton; author and author's agents for 'The Woollen Bank Forgeries' by Keith Waterhouse; The Society of Authors as the literary representative of the Estate of Katherine Mansfield for 'The Doll's House' from *Collected Stories of Katherine Mansfield*.

*Printed in Hong Kong by
Dai Nippon Printing Co (H.K.) Ltd*

CONTENTS

TADDY THE LAMPLIGHTER

Bill Naughton

Through the dense narrow streets where I lived as a boy, there came every evening a man called Taddy the Lamplighter. A bunch of us lads would be huddled round the lamp-post at the corner of Alley Brew, shoving close up to each other for warmth, and telling 'Pat and Mick' tales in the darkness while waiting for him.

From a distance you could see the flicker of his light, held high in the air—fixed in a metal holder at the tip of his long pole—and we would all go silent as he drew near, and our eyes would watch upwards as he turned on the tap with a poke of his pole. The gas would hiss and he would thrust the torchlike tip through the glass door at the bottom of the lamp, and then, at the instant of the bright gaslight exploding over us, we would scatter with cries and cheers of 'Hooray! Good old Taddy!'

Taddy always looked serious, but he seemed to enjoy our applause just the same. He would give a squint at the light, see if it was what it should be, whilst Ollie Baker, a serious-minded sort of lad, would always say something: 'A champion light there tonight, Taddy!' To which Taddy would usually nod: 'Aye, it is that an' all!' Or if the light were not so good Ollie would say: 'Not up to the mark tonight, Taddy!' And Taddy would shake his head and sigh:

'Them 'ometers must be low, me lad.' Then on his way he would go, and Ollie, who was the leader, would decide what game we should play, perhaps 'Jumpy o'er back' or 'Ride or kench.'

One cold December evening there was a very light fall of snow—not enough for snow fights, but enough to make 'a slur'. This was a slide about two feet wide and twenty-five feet in length, starting at the lamp-post and running down the steep pavement of Alley Brew. In swift file we skated down, Ollie leading, and our clog-irons quickly brought up a slippery glass-like surface. And just as we were tiring a bit, Art Baines spotted Taddy's light.

'Quick!' he whispered, 'let's lay a blind slur for Taddy!'

I could see Ollie wasn't for it, but all the others agreed that quick, that he didn't try to sway them. We dropped down on our knees, and with our caps we coaxed a thin coating of snow over our slur. And when it was hidden we got in our usual position by the lamp, and we watched old Taddy as he came along.

His two flat feet slopped up the Brew in the snow, and by some lucky chance they kept just at the edge of the slur without stepping on to it. We had expected him to go arm over tip every step, but he hadn't, and now we watched in silence as he lifted his pole to nudge the tap. Then, just as he was about to pop the torch up the lamp, he moved a foot—and that did for him. He let out a squeak, and in a flurried attempt to recover his balance as his foot slipped, he jerked his other foot on to the slur.

Poor old Taddy—his shout for help was drowned by our laughter and yells as we watched him slide backwards, his pole in the air, and faster he went until he fell flat on his face. And even then, stretched out, he went on sliding, while we ran off with yells and shrieks. But I think we all felt a bit ashamed.

After waiting by the chapel for twenty minutes, and there being no sign of Taddy coming to light his next lamp we got anxious.

'We'll hatta go back an' see,' said Ollie.

There were about nine of us, and with Ollie in the lead we cautiously made our way back.

'Look!' I whispered, 'the owd chap's lying where he fell!'

And sure enough he was, down on the snowy pavement, his pole swung some feet away. He wasn't unconscious, but he was groaning. We went to help him up, expecting him to curse us, but instead he began moaning about the lamps.

'Me lamps!–all me lamps are out!–an' I've busted me arm an' carn't light 'um.' His right arm hung limp. 'Tak' me watch outa m'pocket,' he said. I put my hand in his waistcoat pocket and pulled out a big watch. 'All but eight o'clock,' I said.

'Oh, good grief,' cried Taddy, 'folk won't be able to see their way about without me lamps. I'll get sacked–I will for a surety.'

Ollie stood before the old man:

'We was the instigators, Taddy,' he said solemnly, 'an' it's up to us to see that thy lamps are lit. But first we gotta take thee to Doctor Paddy Bryce to have thy arm fixed.'

'Nay, nay,' said Taddy, brightening up–'the lights come first! I can have my arm fettled afterwards.'

We all marched round with Taddy and his pole,

3

some supporting him, because he felt weak, and others competing for the job of lighting the lamps– which meant a few gas mantles were broken by our excited and inexpert hands. Then we took him to Paddy Bryce's. We gathered outside the doctor's and discussed the situation while he was inside.

'It's not his lighting-up job as is the problem,' said Ollie, 'but his knocking-up job in the morning.'

Taddy combined his job of lamplighter–which was very low paid–with that of knocker-up. Although a number of workers used the newfangled alarum-clock, the majority relied on Taddy. Not only for the human touch but also because Taddy did not merely waken you, he took it as his responsibility to actually get you up. Many with clocks had been known to overlie, but that had never happened to one of Taddy's customers.

'Folk 'ull miss their work,' said Art Baines.

To us, at that time, this seemed the worst thing that could possibly happen to anybody. We all went very quiet, and deadly serious. And when Taddy came out of the surgery, his arm bandaged beneath his topcoat, it was to confirm our fears:

'I'm done,' he said. 'I carn't use my right hand, an' I'll not have strength enough in my left to whack with my knocking-up pole. There'll be eighty-three families miss their work tomorrow–unless a miracle happens.'

'Give us the names an' lend us the pole,' said Ollie, 'an' we'll knock up for thee.'

'No use,' said Taddy with a shake of his head, 'I keep all the names an' times in me head. An' besides that, they every one expect their one special call.

4

They won't get up without it. I've gotta bully some an' coax others, an' so on.'

Ollie turned to me: 'Let's volunteer to go with him in the morning, eh, Bill?'

'It's a late morning,' put in Taddy eagerly. 'My first customer isn't till haw' past four. I could give you both a shout at twenty-past. You could whack an' I'd call.'

Half-past four didn't seem so late to me, but with them all looking at me I had to say I would. But I was uneasy at what my mother would say about being wakened at that hour. To my surprise, however, she agreed with the idea, and since my father was on the night shift I didn't have to worry over him.

The thought of so many families depending on me to get them up worried me out of my sleep, and when Taddy called I was already awake, and I ran downstairs in my bare feet. In two minutes I was dressed and out in the street with a butty in my hand.

'Ollie should be here in a minute,' said Taddy, 'so we'll give Harry Foster a call while we're waiting.'

He handed me a long bamboo pole that had an end made of a fan of flexible wires, and when we got to Foster's I stood looking at the upstairs window, and waiting for Taddy to give me the signal.

'Right, me lad,' he said, 'let him have a tattoo of nice sharp raps, but not too heavy.'

Feeling nervous, but willing, I tapped the wires against the window.

'Nay, nay, that'll never do!' snapped Taddy. 'Sharp raps but not heavy ones.'

The next time I did better, and when I had finished Taddy called up.

5

' 'Arry! 'Arry! it wants a minute to haw-past.'

I heard Harry let out a sigh: 'What time did tha say it were?'

'Haw' past four. Nice morning, 'Arry, a topcoat warmer than it was yes'day. Snow's done it.'

He waited, listening for Harry's footsteps on the bedroom floor. When he heard them clomp heavily he nodded: 'I can trust Harry–he'll not go back to bed. But some of 'um jump straight in again once me back's turned.'

The next customer was Steve Duckley, and Taddy had a change of tactics here. Ollie who had now arrived, was told: 'Keep smattering till tha hears a voice.'

Ollie almost rapped the window in, and both of us laughed because we could hear Steve's snoring above the sound of the wires.

'Steve!' growled Taddy, 'Steve, you flamer–wilt' waken up!'

'Aw . . . aw . . .' grunted Steve.

'Come on,' said Taddy, 'we'll leave him for a few minutes an' go across to Miss Spood who works at the chemic' factory.'

He warned me as I held the pole: 'Very gently, me lad–like it were the breeze playing ont' glass.' Then, after my very delicate tapping he called softly: 'Are you awake, Florence? It's twenty minutes to five, my dear, an' it's a petticoat warmer till it was yes'day.'

Florence replied, 'Yerss!' And as we moved to the next house Taddy explained: 'That girl needs coaxing. She's very sensitive–a sharp word would turn her back into bed for the day.'

The next customer was a miner called Jack Beezer,

6

and I was shocked at the language he used on Taddy. He cursed him for all he was worth, and refused to get up. We went to another customer and then returned to Jack:

'Tha's missed the first winding,' shouted Taddy, 'an' tha's missed the second, an' I'll bet tha misses the third.' Then he whispered to me: 'Keep tapping an' don't stop till I tell thee.' I kept at it, though when Jack jumped up with a roar I ran away.

'He's a good lad is Jack,' said Taddy. 'He allus pays me eightpence a week: fourpence for knocking him up an' fourpence for being cussed by him.'

Twenty minutes later when we were passing Beezer's, Jack was waiting at the door with a pint pot of tea for Taddy. The busiest time was from five-thirty to six-thirty, and after that Taddy relaxed, bought a newspaper, and added an item of news to his greeting:

'Twenty-to-seven, Sarah!' Pause. 'I see they've nabbed that chap who chopped up his wife—he were in lodgings at Blackpoo'.'

Taddy had very sharp eyes and he kept a constant watch for people going back to bed, and if there were no light downstairs he would go back and investigate. Nobody escaped.

At seven o'clock he let Ollie and myself go, saying that he could manage the remaining few without using his pole, and so, excited and slightly tired, we ran off home.

But as the days went on to weeks—and Taddy's arm seemed to get worse instead of better—the job, though interesting, lost most of its excitement. The other lads would go lighting the lamps, but none of them could be relied upon to get up at just after four in the

7

morning, so that the job fell to Ollie and myself all the time.

Then when it seemed that we were destined to go round with Taddy for the rest of our days, it chanced that we bumped into Doctor Bryce one morning–when he was coming out of Ogden's, where the eldest daughter had been having a bad time over her first confinement. He was a very surly chap when sober and it seemed that he was about to pass us without speaking, were it not that he spotted Taddy's arm in the sling.

'What the devil's the matter with you?' he asked. 'It's over a month since I told you to give that arm plenty of exercise.' And being a blunt sort of chap he grabbed Taddy's arm out of the sling and began to shake it violently up and down: 'That's healed grand,' he said, 'so you keep it on the move–or I'll clout your lug if I catch you dodging.'

Ollie and myself saw it all. The minute the doctor walked off Taddy put his hand out for the knocking-up pole.

'An' I should damn well think so!' snorted Ollie.

'Taddy,' I said, 'you're a false 'un!'

'I were lonely,' said Taddy sadly. 'It's a lonely job. You lads were such company for me, I didn't like to be left on my own again. I hope you're not mad at me. Goodbye.'

As we watched him trudge up the street Ollie said: 'Poor chap, his working days are numbered.'

'Why?' I asked.

'They've invented street lights that light themselves,' said Ollie, 'an' them cheap alarum-clocks will soon be all the vogue, so that nob'dy 'ull want a knocker-up.'

8

I half-believed what he said about the lamps, but I could not believe what he said about the clocks. I thought about it walking home in the dark morning, and I could not imagine that any right-minded person would choose to be aroused by the noisy racket of a cheap alarum-clock in preference to Taddy's sensitive window-tapping and his understanding of how folk feel when they're wakened up. By contrast the tin clock seemed a horrible way of being woke up, and I should have been right shaken had I known that it would triumph as swiftly as it did over old Taddy.

2

THE DOLL'S HOUSE

Katherine Mansfield

When dear old Mrs Hay went back to town after staying with the Burnells she sent the children a doll's house. It was so big that the carter and Pat carried it into the court-yard, and there it stayed, propped up on two wooden boxes beside the feed-room door. No harm could come of it; it was summer. And perhaps the smell of paint would have gone off by the time it had to be taken in. For, really, the smell of paint coming from that doll's house ('Sweet of old Mrs Hay, of course; most sweet and generous!')—but the smell of paint was quite enough to make any one seriously ill, in Aunt Beryl's opinion. Even before the sacking was taken off. And when it was . . .

There stood the doll's house, a dark, oily, spinach green, picked out with bright yellow. Its two solid little chimneys, glued on to the roof, were painted red and white, and the door, gleaming with yellow varnish, was like a little slab of toffee. Four windows, real windows, were divided into panes by a broad streak of green. There was actually a tiny porch, too, painted yellow, with big lumps of congealed paint hanging along the edge.

But perfect, perfect little house! Who could possibly mind the smell? It was part of the joy, part of the newness.

'Open it quickly, someone!'

The Hook at the side was stuck fast. Pat prised it open with his penknife, and the whole house-front swung back, and—there you were, gazing at one and the same moment into the drawing-room and dining-room, the kitchen and two bedrooms. That is the way for a house to open! Why don't all houses open like that? How much more exciting than peering through the slit of a door into a mean little hall with a hatstand and two umbrellas! That is—isn't it?—what you long to know about a house when you put your hand on the knocker. Perhaps it is the way God opens houses at dead of night when He is taking a quiet turn with an angel. . . .

'O-oh!' The Burnell children sounded as though they were in despair. It was too marvellous; it was too much for them. They had never seen anything like it in their lives. All the rooms were papered. There were pictures on the walls, painted on the paper, with gold frames complete. Red carpet covered all the floors except the kitchen; red plush chairs in the drawing-room, green in the dining-room; tables, beds with real bedclothes, a cradle, a stove, a dresser with tiny plates and one big jug. But what Kezia liked more than anything, what she liked frightfully, was the lamp. It stood in the middle of the dining-room table, an exquisite little amber lamp with a white globe. It was even filled all ready for lighting, though, of course, you couldn't light it. But there was something inside that looked like oil, and that moved when you shook it.

The father and mother dolls, who sprawled very stiff as though they had fainted in the drawing-room, and their two little children asleep upstairs, were

really too big for the doll's house. They didn't look as though they belonged. But the lamp was perfect. It seemed to smile at Kezia, to say, 'I live here.' The lamp was real.

The Burnell children could hardly walk to school fast enough the next morning. They burned to tell everybody, to describe, to—well—boast about their doll's house before the school-bell rang.

'I'm to tell,' said Isabel, 'because I'm the eldest. And you two can join in after. But I'm to tell first.'

There was nothing to answer. Isabel was bossy, but she was always right, and Lottie and Kezia knew too well the powers that went with being eldest. They brushed through the thick buttercups at the road edge and said nothing.

'And I'm to choose who's to come and see it first. Mother said I might.'

For it had been arranged that while the doll's house stood in the courtyard they might ask the girls at school, two at a time, to come and look. Not to stay to tea, of course, or to come traipsing through the house. But just to stand quietly in the courtyard while Isabel pointed out the beauties, and Lottie and Kezia looked pleased. . . .

But hurry as they might, by the time they had reached the tarred palings of the boys' playground the bell had begun to jangle. They only just had time to whip off their hats and fall into line before the roll was called. Never mind. Isabel tried to make up for it by looking very important and mysterious and by whispering behind her hand to the girls near her, 'Got something to tell you at playtime.'

Playtime came and Isabel was surrounded. The

girls of her class nearly fought to put their arms round her, to walk away with her, to beam flatteringly, to be her special friend. She held quite a court under the huge pine trees at the side of the playground. Nudging, giggling together, the little girls pressed up close. And the only two who stayed outside the ring were the two who were always outside, the little Kelveys. They knew better than to come anywhere near the Burnells.

For the fact was, the school the Burnell children went to was not at all the kind of place their parents would have chosen if there had been any choice. But there was none. It was the only school for miles. And the consequence was all the children in the neighbourhood, the Judge's little girls, the doctor's daughters, the storekeeper's children, the milkman's, were forced to mix together. Not to speak of there being an equal number of rude, rough little boys as well. But the line had to be drawn somewhere. It was drawn at the Kelveys. Many of the children, including the Burnells, were not allowed even to speak to them. They walked past the Kelveys with their heads in the air, and as they set the fashion in all matters of behaviour, the Kelveys were shunned by everybody. Even the teacher had a special voice for them, and a special smile for the other children when Lil Kelvey came up to her desk with a bunch of dreadfully common-looking flowers.

They were the daughters of a spry, hardworking little washerwoman, who went about from house to house by the day. This was awful enough. But where was Mr Kelvey? Nobody knew for certain. But everybody said he was in prison. So they were the daughters of a washer-woman and a gaolbird. Very nice company for other people's children! And they looked it. Why

Mrs Kelvey made them so conspicuous was hard to understand. The truth was they were dressed in 'bits' given to her by the people for whom she worked. Lil, for instance, who was a stout, plain girl, with big freckles, came to school in a dress made from a green art-serge table cloth of the Burnells', with red plush sleeves from the Logans' curtains. Her hat, perched on top of her high forehead, was a grown-up woman's hat, once the property of Miss Lecky, the postmistress. It turned up at the back and was trimmed with a large scarlet quill. What a little guy she looked! It was impossible not to laugh. And her little sister, our Else, wore a long white dress, rather like a nightgown, and a pair of little boy's boots. But whatever our Else wore she would have looked strange. She was a tiny wishbone of a child, with cropped hair and enormous solemn eyes—a little white owl. Nobody had ever seen her smile; she scarcely ever spoke. She went through life holding on to Lil, with a piece of Lil's skirt screwed up in her hand. Where Lil went our Else followed. In the playground, on the road going to and from school, there was Lil marching in front and our Else holding on behind. Only when she wanted anything, or when she was out of breath, our Else gave Lil a tug, a twitch, and Lil stopped and turned round. The Kelveys never failed to understand each other.

Now they hovered at the edge; you couldn't stop them listening. When the little girls turned round and sneered, Lil, as usual, gave her silly, shamefaced smile, but our Else only looked.

And Isabel's voice, so very proud, went on telling. The carpet made a great sensation, but so did the beds with real bedclothes, and the stove with an oven door.

When she finished Kezia broke in. 'You've forgotten the lamp, Isabel.'

'Oh, yes,' said Isabel, 'and there's a teeny little lamp, all made of yellow glass, with a white globe that stands on the dining-room table. You couldn't tell it from a real one.'

'The lamp's best of all,' cried Kezia. She thought Isabel wasn't making half enough of the little lamp. But nobody paid any attention. Isabel was choosing the two who were to come back with them that afternoon and see it. She chose Emmie Cole and Lena Logan. But when the others knew they were all to have a chance, they couldn't be nice enough to Isabel. One by one they put their arms round Isabel's waist and walked her off. They had something to whisper to her, a secret. 'Isabel's *my* friend.'

Only the little Kelveys moved away forgotten; there was nothing more for them to hear.

Days passed, and as more children saw the doll's house, the fame of it spread. It became the one subject, the rage. The one question was, 'Have you seen Burnells' doll's house? Oh, ain't it lovely!' 'Haven't you seen it? Oh, I say!'

Even the dinner hour was given up to talking about it. The little girls sat under the pines eating their thick mutton sandwiches and big slabs of johnny cake spread with butter. While always, as near as they could get, sat the Kelveys, our Else holding on to Lil, listening too, while they chewed their jam sandwiches out of a newspaper soaked with large red blobs. . . .

'Mother,' said Kezia, 'can't I ask the Kelveys just once?''

'Certainly not, Kezia.'

'But why not?'

'Run away, Kezia; you know quite well why not.'

At last everybody had seen it except them. On that day the subject rather flagged. It was the dinner hour. The children stood together under the pine trees, and suddenly, as they looked at the Kelveys eating out of their paper, always by themselves, always listening, they wanted to be horrid to them. Emmie Cole started the whisper.

'Lil Kelvey's going to be a servant when she grows up.'

'O-oh, how awful!' said Isabel Burnell, and she made eyes at Emmie.

Emmie swallowed in a very meaning way and nodded to Isabel as she'd seen her mother do on those occasions.

'It's true—it's true—it's true,' she said.

Then Lena Logan's little eyes snapped. 'Shall I ask her?' she whispered.

'Bet you don't,' said Jessie May.

'Pooh, I'm not frightened,' said Lena. Suddenly she gave a little squeal and danced in front of the other girls. 'Watch! Watch me! Watch me now!' said Lena. And sliding, gliding, dragging one foot, giggling behind her hand, Lena went over to the Kelveys.

Lil looked up from her dinner. She wrapped the rest quickly away. Our Else stopped chewing. What was coming now?

'Is it true you're going to be a servant when you grow up, Lil Kelvey?' shrilled Lena.

Dead silence. But instead of answering, Lil only gave her silly, shamefaced smile. She didn't seem to mind the question at all. What a sell for Lena! The girls began to titter.

Lena couldn't stand that. She put her hands on her hips; she shot forward. 'Yah, yer father's in prison!' she hissed, spitefully.

This was such a marvellous thing to have said that the little girls rushed away in a body, deeply, deeply excited, wild with joy. Someone found a long rope, and they began skipping. And never did they skip so high, run in and out as fast, or do such daring things as on that morning.

In the afternoon Pat called for the Burnell children with the buggy and they drove home. There were visitors. Isabel and Lottie, who liked visitors, went up-stairs to change their pinafores. But Kezia thieved out at the back. Nobody was about; she began to swing on the big white gates of the courtyard. Presently, looking along the road, she saw two little dots. They grew bigger, they were coming towards her. Now she could see that one was in front and one close behind. Now she could see that they were the Kelveys. Kezia stopped swinging. She slipped off the gate as if she was going to run away. Then she hesitated. The Kelveys came nearer, and beside them walked their shadows, very long, stretching right across the road with their heads in the buttercups. Kezia clambered back on the gate; she had made up her mind; she swung out.

'Hullo,' she said to the passing Kelveys.

They were so astounded that they stopped. Lil gave her silly smile. Our Else stared.

'You can come and see our doll's house if you want to,' said Kezia, and she dragged one toe on the ground. But at that Lil turned red and shook her head quickly.

'Why not?' asked Kezia.

Lil gasped, then she said, 'Your ma told our ma you wasn't to speak to us.'

'Oh, well,' said Kezia. She didn't know what to reply. 'It doesn't matter. You can come and see our doll's house all the same. Come on. Nobody's looking.'

But Lil shook her head still harder.

'Don't you want to?' asked Kezia.

Suddenly there was a twitch, a tug at Lil's skirt. She turned round. Our Else was looking at her with big, imploring eyes; she was frowning; she wanted to go. For a moment Lil looked at our Else very doubtfully. But then our Else twitched her skirt again. She started forward. Kezia led the way. Like two little stray cats they followed across the courtyard to where the doll's house stood.

'There it is,' said Kezia.

There was a pause. Lil breathed loudly, almost snorted; our Else was still as a stone.

'I'll open it for you,' said Kezia kindly. She undid the hook and they looked inside.

'There's the drawing-room and the dining-room, and that's the—'

'Kezia!'

Oh, what a start they gave!

'Kezia!'

It was Aunt Beryl's voice. They turned round. At the back door stood Aunt Beryl, staring as if she couldn't believe what she saw.

'How dare you ask the little Kelveys into the court-yard?' said her cold, furious voice. 'You know as well as I do, you're not allowed to talk to them. Run away, children, run away at once. And don't come back again,' said Aunt Beryl. And she stepped into the yard and shooed them out as if they were chickens.

'Off you go immediately!' she called, cold and proud.

They did not need telling twice. Burning with shame, shrinking together, Lil huddled along like her mother, our Else dazed, somehow they crossed the big courtyard and squeezed through the white gate.

'Wicked, disobedient little girl!' said Aunt Beryl bitterly to Kezia, and she slammed the doll's house to.

The afternoon had been awful. A letter had come from Willie Brent, a terrifying, threatening letter, saying if she did not meet him that evening in Pulman's Bush, he'd come to the front door and ask the reason why! But now that she had frightened those little rats of Kelveys and given Kezia a good scolding, her heart felt lighter. The ghastly pressure was gone. She went back to the house humming.

When the Kelveys were well out of sight of Burnells', they sat down to rest on a big red drain-pipe by the side of the road. Lil's cheeks were still burning; she took off the hat with the quill and held it on her knee. Dreamily they looked over the hay paddocks, past the creek, to the group of wattles where Logan's cows stood waiting to be milked. What were their thoughts?

Presently our Else nudged up close to her sister. But now she had forgotten the cross lady. She put out a finger and stroked her sister's quill; she smiled her rare smile.

'I seen the little lamp,' she said, softly.

Then both were silent once more.

3
HA'PENNY

Alan Paton

Of the six hundred boys at the reformatory, about one hundred were from ten to fourteen years of age. My Department had from time to time expressed the intention of taking them away, and of establishing a special institution for them, more like an industrial school than a reformatory. This would have been a good thing, for their offences were very trivial, and they would have been better by themselves. Had such a school been established, I should have liked to be Principal of it myself, for it would have been an easier job; small boys turn instinctively towards affection, and one controls them by it, naturally and easily.

Some of them, if I came near them, either on parade or in school or at football, would observe me watchfully, not directly or fully, but obliquely and secretly; sometimes I would surprise them at it, and make some small sign of recognition, which would satisfy them so that they would cease to observe me, and would give their full attention to the event of the moment. But I knew that my authority was thus confirmed and strengthened.

The secret relations with them were a source of continuous pleasure to me. Had they been my own children I would no doubt have given a greater expression to it. But often I would move through the silent and orderly parade, and stand by one of them. He would look straight in front of him with a little frown of concentration that expressed both childish awareness and manly indifference to my nearness. Sometimes I would tweak his ear, and he would give me a brief smile of acknowledgement, or frown with still greater concentration. It was natural, I suppose, to confine these outward expressions to the very smallest, but they were taken as symbolic, and some older boys would observe them and take themselves to be included. It was a relief, when the reformatory was passing through times of turbulence and trouble, and when there was danger of estrangement between authority and boys, to make those simple and natural gestures, which were reassurances to both me and them that nothing important had changed.

On Sunday afternoons when I was on duty I would take my car to the reformatory and watch the free boys being signed out at the gate. This simple operation was watched by many boys not free, who would tell each other, 'In so many weeks I'll be signed out myself.' Among the watchers were always some of the small boys, and these I would take by turns in the car. We would go out to the Potchefstroom Road with its ceaseless stream of traffic, and to the Baragwanath crossroads, and come back by the Van Wyksrus road to the reformatory. I would talk to them about their families, their parents, their sisters and brothers, and I would pretend to know nothing of Durban, Port Elizabeth, Potchefstroom, and Clocolan, and ask them if these places were bigger than Johannesburg.

One of the small boys was Ha'penny, and he was about twelve years old. He came from Bloemfontein and was the biggest talker of them all. His mother worked in a white person's house, and he had two brothers and two sisters. His brothers were Richard and Dickie, and his sisters Anna and Mina.

'Richard and Dickie?' I asked.

'Yes, meneer.'

'In English,' I said, 'Richard and Dickie are the same name.'

When we returned to the reformatory, I sent for Ha'penny's papers; there it was plainly set down, Ha'penny was a waif, with no relatives at all. He had been taken in from one home to another, but he was naughty and uncontrollable, and eventually had taken to pilfering at the market.

I then sent for the Letter Book, and found that Ha'penny wrote regularly, or rather that others wrote for him till he could write himself, to Mrs Betty Maarman, of 48 Vlak Street, Bloemfontein. But Mrs Maarman had never once replied to him. When questioned, he had said, perhaps she is sick. I sat down and wrote at once to the Social Welfare Officer at Bloemfontein, asking him to investigate.

The next time I had Ha'penny out in the car I questioned him again about his family. And he told me the same as before, his mother, Richard and Dickie, Anna and Mina. But he softened the 'D' of Dickie, so that it sounded now like Tickie.

'I thought you said Dickie,' I said.

'I said Tickie,' he said.

He watched me with concealed apprehension, and I came to the conclusion that this waif of Bloemfontein was a clever boy, who had told me a story that was all imagination, and had changed one single letter of it to make it safe from any question. And I thought I understood it all too, that he was ashamed of being

23

without a family and had invented them all, so that no one might discover that he was fatherless and motherless and that no one in the world cared whether he was alive or dead. This gave me a strong feeling for him, and I went out of my way to manifest towards him that fatherly care that the State, though not in those words, had enjoined upon me by giving me this job.

Then the letter came from the Social Welfare Officer in Bloemfontein, saying that Mrs Betty Maarman of 48 Vlak Street was a real person, and that she had four children, Richard and Dickie, Anna and Mina, but that Ha'penny was no child of her, and she knew him only as a derelict of the streets. She had never answered his letters, because he wrote to her as 'Mother', and she was no mother of his, nor did she wish to play any such role. She was a decent woman, a faithful member of the church, and she had no thought of corrupting her family by letting them have anything to do with such a child.

But Ha'penny seemed to me anything but the usual delinquent; his desire to have a family was so strong, and his reformatory record was so blameless, and his anxiety to please and obey so great, that I began to feel a great duty towards him. Therefore I asked him about his 'mother'.

He could not speak enough of her, nor with too high praise. She was loving, honest, and strict. Her home was clean. She had affection for all her children. It was clear that the homeless child, even as he had attached himself to me, would have attached himself to her; he had observed her even as he had observed me, but did not know the secret of how to open her heart, so that she would take him in, and save him from the lonely life that he led.

'Why did you steal when you had such a mother?' I asked.

He could not answer that; not all his brains nor his courage could find an answer to such a question, for he knew that with such a mother he would not have stolen at all.

'The boy's name is Dickie,' I said, 'not Tickie.'

And then he knew the deception was revealed. Another boy might have said, 'I told you it was Dickie,' but he was too intelligent for that; he knew that if I had established that the boy's name was Dickie, I must have established other things too. I was shocked by the immediate and visible effect of my action. His whole brave assurance died within him, and he stood there exposed, not as a liar, but as a homeless child who had surrounded himself with mother, brothers, and sisters, who did not exist. I had shattered the very foundations of his pride, and his sense of human significance.

He fell sick at once, and the doctor said it was tuberculosis. I wrote at once to Mrs Maarman, telling her the whole story, of how this small boy had observed her, and had decided that she was the person he desired for his mother. But she wrote back saying that she could take no responsibility for him. For one thing, Ha'penny was a Mosuto, and she was a coloured woman; for another, she had never had a child in trouble, and how could she take such a boy?

Tuberculosis is a strange thing; sometimes it manifests itself suddenly in the most unlikely host, and swiftly sweeps to the end. Ha'penny withdrew himself from the world, from all Principals and mothers, and the doctor said there was little hope. In desperation I sent money for Mrs Maarman to come.

She was a decent, homely woman, and, seeing that the situation was serious, she, without fuss or embarrassment, adopted Ha'penny for her own. The whole reformatory accepted her as his mother. She sat the whole day with him, and talked to him of Richard and Dickie, Anna and Mina, and how they were all waiting for him to come home. She poured out her affection on him, and had no fear of his sickness, nor did she allow it to prevent her from satisfying his hunger to be owned. She talked to him of what they would do when he came back, and how he would go to school, and what they would buy for Guy Fawkes night.

He in his turn gave his whole attention to her, and when I visited him he was grateful, but I had passed out of his world. I felt judged in that I had sensed only the existence and not the measure of his desire. I wished I had done something sooner, more wise, more prodigal.

We buried him on the reformatory farm, and Mrs Maarman said to me, 'When you put up the cross, put he was my son.'

'I'm ashamed,' she said, 'that I wouldn't take him.'

'The sickness,' I said, 'the sickness would have come.'

'No,' she said, shaking her head with certainty. 'It wouldn't have come. And if it had come at home, it would have been different.'

So she left for Bloemfontein, after her strange visit to a reformatory. And I was left too, with the resolve to be more prodigal in the task that the State, though not in so many words, had enjoined upon me.

4
THE SHAFT

Sid Chaplin

Williamson looked up from the bunch of reports he was reading. Although he smiled around the lips, his eyes were worried.

'Sit down, Harry,' he said. 'Ah'll get through these first.' Harry sat down uneasily, rumpling his cap. Williamson went on with his pretence of reading the reports. There came another knock at the office door. Both men turned. Williamson put the reports carefully on to the desk. 'Come in!' he called out.

The man who entered could have been Harry's double. There was the same solid, medium build and sandy hair. Blue eyes set in a square face. A hard, uncompromising mouth. His eyes darted from Williamson to Harry, then back to Williamson. 'Morning, Mr Williamson,' he said. There was a strain of reproach mingling with the respect in his voice. 'Good morning, Willy,' Williamson said. 'Find a seat.' Willy found a seat, as far away from Harry as was possible.

Harry stood up. His lips were one thin bitter line. 'Ah daresay our business can wait, Mr Williamson. Ah'll be at hand when ye want me.' He made for the door. Williamson sighed. This was going to be a tough job. 'You can sit down again, Harry. Ah want a word with both of ye.' He leaned back in his chair and tried to assume confidence.

'You'll both be wondering why Ah've asked you to call here today, eh?' Both men shifted uncomfortably.

'Well, it's awkward, dam' awkward, but it's got to
stop, see? Seems everybody knew about this but me, or
you'd have been on the carpet before now. What you
do outside of work isn't any concern of mine, but when
two men on a job like yours aren't on speaking terms,
it's time to draw the line.' His eyes roved from the
ceiling to the two silent men. Both stared back with
rising hostility.

'What's the grumble,' asked Willy. 'We're keeping
the shafts good; we do our work proper; so with all
due respect to you, Mr Williamson, Ah think you're
out of order.'

Williamson waved a placatory hand. 'No grumbles
about your work; none, none at all. But this is what
Ah'm getting at. You two don't speak? Right? Well,
it's none of my business why, but remember you're on a
responsible job. And accidents can happen in them
shafts. Ah've seen one or two in my time. Accidents,
mind ye. And what's people going to say if anything
does happen to one of ye, eh?'

There was a long silence. 'We know our work,' said
Harry at last. 'Nothing's going to happen.'

'It's between him and me,' said Willy. 'Personal;
nothing to do with work, or with you.'

'That's right,' said Harry. 'It's our affair and ye
needn't worry about it interfering with our work.'

Williamson thumped the table. 'My God!' he cried.
'Are ye men, or just bits of bairns? Can't ye see what
Ah'm getting at? With the best will in the world anything can happen in a pit-shaft. . . .' As he spoke the
words a sudden terrifying vision flashed across his
mind. He saw two hundred fathoms of shaft vertically
piercing the strata; a shadowy hole diminishing into

extreme blackness. He saw the pipe-lined sides; pipes sucking unending gallons of water from underground dams; pipes carrying electric cables, and pipes through which rushed air, compressed to drive a thousand drills through virgin coal and naked rock. He saw the greasy black cables of the guides quiver like the key-cable of a web when a fly is enmeshed, and then a cage flash by with two figures on top, two men holding to the guy chains almost nonchalantly.

He switched his mind to the office; he had seen that picture a few times in the last few days; and always with a singularly sinister ending. Williamson possessed an imagination.

He raked both men with a significant glance. 'So it's got to stop! You can cut each other dead in the street, but by God, you'll speak at work! Either that, or one of you goes. That's final.' He fumbled with his reports. Both men remained seated dumbly staring at him. 'That's all,' he said.

They walked out. Through his office window he saw them turn in opposite directions. A pity, he thought, two good workmen and brothers at that. Brothers! Well, they're not doing a Cain and Abel on this job. Give them a week, no more. Then one of them goes. Or both for that matter. That one or the other might capitulate never entered his mind. Williamson knew his men.

When Harry got home he found his wife busy with rolling pin and dough, baking fadges and red with the fire's heat. A neat little woman with sharp features enclosed by a mop of hair which had earned for her the nick-name of Ma Golliwog among the local bairns. 'Well?' she asked sharply. 'And what did Mr

Williamson want with ye?'

He settled down gloomily in the big rocking-chair. 'Come to his ears about me an' Willy never speaking. Says it won't do.' She slammed the rolling pin on to the table. 'Well, Ah'll be jiggered! A fine thing it is when the bosses start interfering with the men's family affairs. It won't do, eh? Well, it'll have to do, 'cos Ah'll nivver speak to that lot again! And Mr Williamson can like it or lump it.'

She picked up her rolling pin and started to stamp, rather than roll, the unhappy dough. Then she looked up suspiciously. 'And what had you to say to him?'

'Told him it was our affair, and so did Willy.'

'Willy? Ye don't mean to tell me that he had ye both there? The impudence of the man!' she screeched, her eyes flashing fire.

'Said that if we don't settle the thing he's going to sack one of us.'

'Well, now, Harry Ward,' she said, quiet now, 'if you start speaking to that brother of yours, Ah'll leave you. So that's that.'

'Catch me speaking to him,' he said. 'Ah'll not forget him in a hurry.' But as he rocked the old chair he got to wondering how that slight seven stone of woman could hold so much bitterness. He sighed, then lit his pipe.

At the other side of the village much the same scene occurred at the home of Willy Ward. Willy may have been a little gloomier and his wife a trifle more bitter. After hearing the story, she repeated her determination not to patch up the quarrel, come what might. 'But what if Ah lose me job, honey?' said Willy. 'Might easily be me that has to go.'

'It'll not be you,' said his wife, confidently. 'You're twice as good a man as him. So you're not going to be first to break silence. Not after the way they carried on the day your Dad was buried. And all because he left them pictures to you. Not that they're very good pictures, they're not, and if it wasn't for the principle of the thing Ah'd let them have them. But there it is; the will was read, it was there in black and white for all the world to see! And then that screaming vulgar Lizzie had to start shoutin' at the top of her voice that they'd been promised to her. The very idea! No, it was them that started it and they shall finish it. D'ye hear what Ah say, Willy Ward?'

'Aye,' answered her husband, and went to bed for some sleep and peace. When he awoke the room was dark. A rattling window told of a high wind outside. He lay a moment, wishing he had another job and could lie in bed o' nights, instead of going out to work when others were going to sleep. Then he remembered the interview with Williamson and realised that his wish might soon come true. Groaning, he got out of bed and made his way downstairs. His supper was laid ready for him 'Bit of a wind up,' he remarked. 'Aye, it's blown tiles off every roof in the street. And Mrs Roberts come in to say that the roof's been blown off the tin chapel!'

He had his supper and set off for work after another warning that there was to be no pact 'unless he speaks first'.

It *was* a wind! It billowed his raincoat out like a balloon and blew him, almost carried him, to the pit. Several times tiles and slates whizzed past his head to splinter into a thousand pieces at his feet. He was glad when he got to work. Harry was already in their cabin, changing into the warm, heavy clothes and buckling on his safety straps and belt. On a slate was chalked their work for that night. 'Loose guides in No. 1 shaft. Burst water-pipe in No. 2.' He glanced at the slate and proceeded to change.

It wasn't necessary to discuss which job should be done first. The burst pipe took precedence, since it would take longer to repair. Willy changed while Harry collected the gear needed. Not a word was said. When they went out the wind was blowing a gale. Harry was first out and he was swept back into the cabin like a ninepin, almost knocking Willy on to his back. There was no apology given, or expected.

They struggled against the wind until they reached 'the hole' at the base of the headstocks, then passed through an air-lock and entered the steel superstructure which covered the shaft. There they stood a moment, watching the cages sweep past with their cargoes of coal. Finally the electric bell above their heads shrilled six times. A door on the landing-level above them opened and the banksman appeared. 'All clear down there,' he shouted. Both men nodded. Used to their ways, he descended the spider-ladder to the duplicate controls.

'She's a raw, rough wind tonight,' he said. 'Aye she's rough,' said Harry. He tightened his safety-belt one hole. Worry had kept him from eating since the interview with Williamson. Davies rapped the cage to the level of the hole. It glided slowly into view, glistening wet with the sprayed water from the burst. The shaft-men stepped on to the roof, fastened their safety-belts to the guy-chains, hung the gong, their only method of communication with Davies, then switched on their cap-lamps.

'Ready?' asked Davies. The wailing of the wind above, striking music from the pulley-wheels and girders, made him uneasy. There was something about the two men, also, that made for uneasiness, the way they walked, with a flicker of an eyelid, or a motion of the hand. 'It's not natural,' he muttered. 'Brothers at that!' He watched intently, waiting for a nod from each. Each man took hold of the nearest guy-chain, then nodded.

He rapped away and watched the cage slowly sink into the black hole until it disappeared. Then, attaching the chain of the manual-signal to his hand, he walked to the edge of the shaft and peered down. He saw the two figures on the cage-top, curiously foreshortened in the glow of their lamps, like men viewed through the wrong end of a telescope. Indeed, the shaft itself, with its diminishing wet walls, was like the inside of a gigantic telescope. The gong sounded. Its peal came echoing out of the depths, faint against the background of the gale that raged outside. He pulled the manual-chain urgently and sighed with relief as the greasy black steel ropes came to a standstill.

Down below, the cage was level with the burst pipe. A stream of water was sprayed from it, and the two men were soon soaked. They had a pair of clamps ready, but the pipe was out of reach when their safety-belts were attached, so they unfastened them, and proceeded to fix the clamps.

Harry had the inner clamp, and this meant he had to lie on the cage-top, holding his clamp in position with one hand while he held on to a guy-chain with the other, and Willy attached the other clamp and bolted it. It was an uncomfortable job for Harry, since the dripping water was ice-cold and his arm ached with the weight of the clamp.

And it was just at this moment that the gale above reached its peak, dislodging a rusting, insecure section of corrugated iron roofing. The wind lifted it as if it were no heavier than a sheet of newspaper, and pitched it unerringly into the narrow outlet of the superstructure. It swept past the astonished Davies and entered the shaft, ricocheting from side to side. The two men heard it coming. Harry pulled himself back on to his knees, letting the clamp drop. It crashed to the shaft-bottom, followed a split-second later by the section of roofing, which brushed, just brushed, Harry in passing.

But it was enough to knock him off his balance, and he would have followed clamp and roof-section had not Willy, by a purely reflex action, which was perfectly timed, caught him by the wrist. Harry's thirteen stone pulled Willy to the roof of the cage, but he still managed to hold on, with both hands clamped around one of Harry's wrists. He tried to pull his brother back, but found he was in no position for lifting; indeed, he imagined he heard his arms scrape in their sockets with the downward pull. Harry's dead-white face gazed up at him, running with sweat and water mixed. For the burst pipe was spraying directly above their heads. And, kick as hard as he could, Harry could not find even a bolt-head to support himself upon.

There was only one thing to do and that was to get the cage back to the level where Davies could help. But the gong was well out of reach. He locked one of his feet round a guy-chain and tried to kick out at the gong with the other. But it was too far away. There was only one thing left to do. He shouted. The Bull of Bashan had nothing on Willy that night. His desperate yell floated out of the blackness, and Davies, leaning over the shaft edge, heard it above the gale. '*Raise her to bank, Joe!*'

Davies pulled the manual chain and watched the sliding ropes, with his heart pounding. When the cage came into view he saw the situation immediately. He rapped hold and leaped on to grab the other arm. Even so, the two of them had a struggle to haul Harry back to safety. For a full five minutes all three lay on the cage-top, panting for breath. Then Willy stood up. The other brother tried to follow suit but failed.

'Take it easy, now,' said Willy. Harry looked up. He had not heard that voice for months; he had not heard that particular note in it since they were lads together, the day he'd fallen in the river and lost a stocking, and Willy had met him going home, crying his eyes out. Then he smiled slowly. 'Always knew you'd be the one to break t'silence,' he said.

Willy had no immediate answer for this. His mind was on those few minutes of agony in the shaft. He had seen one man fall the full two hundred fathoms; he had seen the shattered, shapeless body wrapped in canvas. The Missus can play hell about me speaking first, he thought. Imagine Harry, me brother, lying down there, dead and broken. But he's alive, and Ah'd suffer a thousand nagging women for the joy of it.

'Mebbe Ah did break silence,' he said, 'but some-body had to speak, and since thou was so shook wi' fear, and Joe was out of breath a bit, it had to be me.'

THE WOOLLEN BANK FORGERIES

Keith Waterhouse

When I was nine years old I developed an insane passion for a cricket set on Woolworth's toy counter. This was in the days when everything at Woollie's cost either threepence or sixpence. Sixpence for the bat, ball sixpence, stumps sixpence, bails threepence, pads sixpence apiece, analysis book threepence, total three shillings. I made up my mind that I was going to have the cricket set. Long before I worked out how I was going to steal the money I was rehearsing what I would say to my mother when I took the gear home for the first time.

'No, only they've started a cricket team in our class. And do you know who's got to look after all the stuff, mam? Me.'

Immediate suspicion. 'How do you mean, you've got to look after it? Why can't they look after their own stuff?'

'Ah well, it's not really a school team, it's just our teacher. Old Webby, Mr Webb. He sees us all playing cricket in the street with an old tennis ball, so he says we could start our own team up in that field, and all look after the stuff in turns. He said we shouldn't be playing in the street.'

'Yes, and I've told you not to play in the street as well.'

My mother, with her flat damp voice, was so predictable that I could make up whole conversations with her before I got into the house, examining and re-examining each statement for flaws, leading myself up my own garden path and reconnoitring for trip-wires.

'Who paid out for it, then?'

'Mr Webb. He paid out for it himself.'

'What's *he* want to buy you cricket things for?' And so on.

First I had to get the money. I had several sources of income, but none large enough to get three shillings together at one go. The blue cup on the panshelf where she kept the pennies for the gas, that was worth two-pence at one swoop, or perhaps threepence, depending on how full it was, but never more. Or the fish and chips: by buying twopennyworth instead of three-pennyworth I could save a penny, but it was a risk. She always knew.

I thought for a long time that she had someone down there in the fish shop who ran back and told her what I'd bought.

'How many chips did you get?'

'Threepennorth.'

'How many chips did you get?'

'Three pennorth.'

'How—many—chips—did—you—get?'

'Told you, threepennorth.'

'You didn't get threepennorth at all. You got two-pennorth. Didn't you?'

'No.'

'Didn't you?'

'No.'

'*Did*n't you?'

'Yes.'

'Where's that penny?'

'What penny?'

'I'll give you what penny, my lad! What have you done with it?'

'Lost it!'

'You didn't lose it at all. You've spent it! Have you spent it? You can't keep your hands off nothing, can you?'

I got sixpence a month from the church for singing in the choir, and threepence to take to the Wolf Cubs on Friday night towards the excursion to the Zoo. And sixpence on Monday morning to take to school and put in the bank. And twopence milk money, which I spent on myself as a matter of course.

Bank day was the big ceremony of the week. Each one of us at school had a little, green, linen-backed bank book, and on Monday mornings we paid in our sixpences or, in some rare cases, shillings and even half-crowns, to the Woollen Bank. The teacher acted as agent or collector for the bank. We started first thing, after the attendance register had been called. Webby would call out the names again, in a different order for some obscure reason, and this time we would march up in turn and pay out our money and have it entered in our little green books.

'Littlewood?'

'Here, sir.'

'Yes, we can see you're here, Littlewood. Where's your bank money?'

'Forgot it, sir.'

'You'd forget your head if it was loose, wouldn't you, Littlewood? All right. Patterson?'

'Sir.'

It cut very nicely into the geography class.

Some boys drew their money out regularly every four or five weeks, in florins and half-crowns, whenever their fathers were on short time; and some never had anything in the bank at all except an erratic sixpence on the wrong side of Christmas.

My own account usually went up to ten or twelve shillings before my mother made me draw it out to buy a pair of boots or something, and then we would start again at sixpence a week.

'Parker?'

'Sir.'

'Richards?'

'Drawing out, sir.'

'You're always drawing out, Richards.'

I had nothing in the bank. A neat red double line marked the last withdrawal and the new boots were squeaky on my feet. A sixpence screwed up in newspaper was ready to start the account again.

'Newbould.'

'Sir.'

'Well, move yourself, Newbould.'

'Haven't anything to put in, sir.'

'Why not?'

'My mother says we can't afford it this week, sir.'

'All right, Newbould.–Baker?'

'Sir.'

'Jordan?'

'Sir.'

I had sixpence in my pocket, wrapped up in a piece torn from the *Argus*. The first shiver ran down my back as I imagined dropping it in the playground and Webby recognising it as bank money.

'It's what my mother gave me to get a cut loaf, sir.'

39

Five more like this would make three shillings. Two-pence milk money would pay the tram fare to and from Woollie's.

'Here, why hasn't Mr Webb filled your bank book up?'

'Eh? Oh, he doesn't, sometimes. He sometimes leaves it till the end of the month.'

'Well, that's a funny way of doing it. How does he know how much you've paid in?'

'Ah, well, he's got a big book with it all written down.'

I never got the cricket set. On the way home from school, going the long way round while I worked out full and detailed dialogues with my mother about the bank book, I passed the Chocolate Cabin, the sweet-shop belonging to the Regal cinema. In the little side window there was always a card advertising this or that assortment, and today there was a new card all about Ascot Royal, the new quarter-pound selection box. I went in and bought it, a box slightly smaller than the dummy in the window, and told them it was for my mother's birthday.

I ate the chocolates in quick bites all the way home. I never knew there were so many in a quarter of a pound. Even accounting for the bits of chocolate-coloured straw in three corners, I couldn't eat them all. I had five left when I approached our street. I put two in a privet hedge, gave one away to a little girl who was playing in her vest at the side of the road, and carried two home. I told my mother Mr Webb had given them to me.

'What's he want to give you chocolates for?'

'I don't know. He gave us all two each out of a big box.'

'He must have more money than sense.'

The sixpences slid slowly by. The second one I spent on my way to school on sugared almonds, which I had always fancied. The third one I kept until night and then went to the Regal and saw a film about a train in which the carriage door opens and someone throws a severed hand into the compartment.

I have dreamt about it since but I did not dream about it then, although I would lie awake wondering what was going to happen about the bank money. The fourth one I spent on an enormous wood-fibre scribbling block and told my mother that the rag and bone man was giving them away outside our school. The fifth sixpence was rolled away in pennies at a small and shoddy fair that halted for the day on some waste ground.

When I had got through two and sixpence my mother looked in the bank book. It was bound to happen sooner or later, and each Monday morning when she gave the book to me and each Monday dinnertime when I handed it back, another sixpence spent, I would jump small hurdles of apprehension, my eyes scouring her face for traces of suspicion and my ears strained to catch faint lilts of accusation in her voice.

It was, as a matter of fact, on a Wednesday. She had been going on about my wearing down the heels of my new boots and as usual she went on to drag up some other topic. My mother was too tired for spontaneous wrath. The graver sins were always hoarded until she could launch her rage with the touch-paper of some pettier misdemeanour.

'And another thing, why hasn't Mr Webb filled in your bank book?'

It suddenly seemed ridiculous that she had only now got round to asking about it.

'Eh? Oh, he doesn't sometimes. He sometimes leaves it till the end of the month.'

'How do you mean, he leaves it to the end of the month? Of course he doesn't leave it to the end of the month.'

'Ah no, but he's started doing, because he's got 2B's books to do as well. So he like collects them and fills them in at the end of the month.

'Have you been paying that money in?'

'Eh? course I've been paying it in, what do you think I've been doing with it? He just marks it up every month, that's all.'

'Well, there's five weeks here not marked up. If I find out you've taken that money yourself...'

'Course I haven't taken it, what do I want with it?' I had rehearsed this too. I had rehearsed it, under the sweating blankets, every inch of the way to the reformatory. 'He just hasn't marked it up. He's got a big book and he puts it in that.'

'Well, he can just take it out again. Because I'm drawing it out. You can just get that money drawn out on Monday. Because I need it. And you can just tell him to mark that book in future.

'I've told him. He doesn't take any notice.'

'He will take notice if I go down to that school.'

I prayed. Please God, get me out of this one and don't let her count the gas money on the panshelf, then I'll be all right.

It was a question of two and six. Better than letting it drag on until there was ten shillings to find, or twelve shillings. At the back of my mind I had already

43

planned where the money was coming from. The Cub excursion to the Zoo was about eight weeks off. The full cost of the outing was five shillings, and there was three shillings so far in the kitty.

On Friday, while a game of British Bulldog was going on, I straightened my jersey and sought out Baloo at the back of the hall and told her I would not be going on the excursion.

'Why not?'

'My mother says we can't afford it.'

'But it's only threepence a week. Surely she can spare threepence a week?'

'No, it's not that, miss. She wants to draw out what we've put in already. To get a shirt.'

Baloo gave me her keen social worker's glance but I was not afraid of that.

' 'Cos I've only got one shirt and it's all torn.'

'Well, it's a shame. It's only another two shillings and you'd have enough to go on the trip.'

'I know. She says I can go another year.'

At the end of the evening, after Taps, Baloo put the three shillings in a clean envelope and handed it over. I kept it in my pocket and worried all night in case my mother went through my trousers and found it.

'What's this money?'

'Eh? Oh, it's what I drew out of the bank for you. Forgot to tell you, they always pay out on Fridays now.'

'Well you only had two and six in. What's this extra?'

'Interest.'

On Saturday morning I spent my last sixpence on toffee, reducing the sum to half a crown. On Saturday afternoon, when my mother was over at the cemetery

I got out the blue ink and the red ink and got to work on the bank book.

It wasn't a bad forgery. First of all I added five sixpences together, copying five consecutive Mondays' dates from the doggy calendar by the mantelpiece. And then, carefully tracing an imitation of Webby's scrawl, I put 'Withdrn.—2s 6d'. Drew a double red line under it, as he did. Blotted it. Panicked, at the sudden realisation that my mother might look at the bank book again before Monday. Prayed. Burned the blotting paper and disturbed the ash with the poker so that she could not fish it out and decipher what I had written.

At Monday dinnertime she got her half-crown and her bank book back. She glanced at the green book perfunctorily and put it away for ever. I had already decided to lose it down the fever drain if she ever opened that account again. I went out into the yard and stood on my hands against the lavatory door, for pleasure, and it was Friday, Cub night, before the gnawing fears began again and I began to wonder what would happen if she ever ran into Baloo.

I spent the threepence she gave me for the Zoo excursion. I was having some very rich weeks. I had a feeling that when it came to it they might take me on the excursion for nothing, out of charity, and my only worry as the weeks passed was whether Baloo would call at the house and put this proposition to my mother.

'Just come in here. Now then. What have you done with all that money I gave you to give Miss Dickinson?'

But when the last Friday came there was no question of it. They made their elaborate arrangements, to meet for the long trip at the Corn Exchange at seven in the morning with a packed dinner and a packed tea, and to go to the lavatory before they got on the coach.

I was up at six on Saturday morning and in my uniform, neckerchief straight, green garter tabs in position, by half-past. My last fear was that my mother would insist on taking me to the Corn Exchange. But she gave me my meals in a large brown paper bag, twopence for the tram fare and twopence for myself, and kissed me, I should think for the first time since I was in my pram. I went slowly up the empty street with sevenpence in my pocket–fourpence from my mother and threepence the last instalment on the zoo money– planning the long day and marvelling at the cold brightness of the workman's morning.

I went to the park where the gates were still locked, climbed the railings and had the lake to myself to walk round twenty times before the ranger appeared in the distance and I ran into the woods nearby where the ferns were still wet. I sat for a long time on a green bench and ate the first sandwich, cheese and onion, from my paper bag. I went from tree to tree, counting a hundred by each one before moving on. I nearly slept in the long grass. I took a piece of stone and tried to scrape my initials in the old men's shelter and then took fright and ran away again. The sandwiches were finished and I was down to the bun and the apple.

At the top of the hill on the edge of the woods, at the far side of the park, I stopped at the ramshackle wooden shop and bought some liquorice bootlaces and a twopenny chocolate whirl. I sat on the long low wall by the side of the road and eventually a man came by and stopped and turned round and gave me the Wolf Cub salute. Shyly, without getting up, I put my own two fingers and saluted him back.

'I'm the Akela of the 23rd South-east Pack. What's your Pack?'

'Twenty-second North-east, sir.'

'And where are they?'

'They've gone off to Manchester for the day, sir, to the zoo. Only my mother wouldn't let me go.'

He moved off and full of guilt I went back into the woods and walked around the trees while the day wore on.

When the sky was getting dark and I was tired, I set off home slowly, the longest way, sometimes walking backwards to waste the last half hour, and rehearsing what I would say to my mother. The street was empty again. My mother was in the kitchen, washing clothes and straining her eyes in the gloom to save the light. I flopped down on the buffet by the empty fire and waited for her to speak so that I could discover what she knew.

'Just look at you! Where've you been?'

'Zoo, where do you think I've been?'

'I'd have thought you'd been down the pit to look at you. You're black bright! Just look at your jersey.'

For the first time I examined my clothes, stained with grass and tree-bark, my boots streaked with white where the dew had dried on them, my hands and knees lined with rust where I had stood so long gripping the railings round the woods, remembering what I had read or seen at the Regal about zoos.

'Well, it's mucky, is the zoo. We sat down on some grass for a picnic.'

'You look as though you've been sat down in a coal cellar.'

47

'Hey, mam, did you know elephants squirt water at each other when they have a bath?'

'You look as though *you* need a bath, never mind the elephants.'

'Well they do, they squirt each other. And we saw all these monkeys having a party.'

'Anyone'd think you were a monkey to look at you. And what's that tear in your trousers?'

I kept her talking, giving her opportunities to accuse me if she wanted to, but there was no more than routine disapproval in her voice. I told her about the zebras, the camel, the seals catching fish and the chimpanzee that stole a schoolboy's cap and ran away with it. She rubbed at my face and knees with a cold flannel caked in soap and listened to all I had to say. At the end she said:

'And who said you could give that tip-up lorry away to Jackie Hardcastle?'

'I didn't give it to him. I only lent it to him.'

'Well you can just stop lending things. And you get it back tomorrow morning. And don't you lend out things again.'

I went to bed and undressed in the dark. I slept and in the morning it was Sunday and I went to church. I still had three pennies left out of my sevenpence. I put them on the collection plate, for my criminal career was over. I was glad she had found out about the tip-up lorry, and for the first time in many months I had no fears at all. I was going to stop stealing the gas-money.

In the robing room, one of the other choirboys spoke to me.

'Hey, Newbouldy, where had you been yesterday afternoon in your Cub clothes?'

'When?'

'Yesterday, when do you think? You hadn't been on that zoo excursion, I know that much, because they didn't come back till ten o'clock last night.'

'Where did you see me, then? On the golf-links?'

'No, in your street. You were just going home.'

I felt the low, watery thud at the bottom of my stomach. Struggling out of my surplice I said. 'What time was it?'

'Don't ask me, kid. 'Bout half past twelve. One o'clock. When it got right dark. Just before it started pelting down with rain.'

I ran all the way home, almost crying, and too seized with fear to rehearse any explanations about being sent home early from the zoo by special coach. I had time to wonder why I hadn't thought to come down this way, past the church, and see the time by the old clock. Half-remembered snatches of the previous night's talking darted through my head, and it seemed now that her words had been larded with suspicion and disbelief, and that she was just waiting for some little incident to spark her off into the grand recrimination.

'Why did you tell me you'd been on that excursion?'

'What excursion?'

'I'll give you what excursion before I've finished, my lad.'

But in the house everything was quiet. She was making Yorkshire puddings and she even asked me if I would like to stir the batter, a great favour.

I tested her, deliberately talking about the zoo and giving her a chance to contradict me.

'Hey, the Scouts are going to that zoo next month

49

as well. Where we went to.'

'Never mind the Scouts, just watch what you're doing.'

'I bet their coach doesn't go as fast as ours. It didn't half go fast. We were there in no time.'

'Just watch what you're doing.'

I created the little incident, giving her an opening to get on to the bigger issues; I splashed batter over the clean newspapers that lined the kitchen table. But she only said: 'You're going to have that on the floor if you don't stop your chattering and watch what you're doing.'

I tested her and tested her for a week before I let the subject drop. And she never said anything. A fortnight later she met Baloo while she was out shopping and had a long talk with her. I tested her again about the zoo. But she never said anything.

6

THROUGH THE TUNNEL

Doris Lessing

Going to the shore on the first morning of the holiday,
the young English boy stopped at a turning of the path
and looked down at a wild and rocky bay, and then
over to the crowded beach he knew so well from other
years. His mother walked on in front of him, carrying a
bright-striped bag in one hand. Her other arm, swinging loose, was very white in the sun. The boy watched
that white, naked arm, and turned his eyes, which had
a frown behind them, toward the bay and back again
to his mother. When she felt he was not with her, she
swung around. 'Oh, there you are, Jerry!' she said. She
looked impatient, then smiled. 'Why, darling, would
you rather not come with me? Would you rather—'.
She frowned, conscientiously worrying over what
amusements he might secretly be longing for which she
had been too busy or too careless to imagine. He was
very familiar with that anxious, apologetic smile. Contrition sent him running after her. And yet, as he ran,
he looked back over his shoulder at the wild bay; and
all morning, as he played on the safe beach, he was
thinking of it.

Next morning, when it was time for the routine of
swimming and sunbathing, his mother said, 'Are you
tired of the usual beach, Jerry? Would you like to go
somewhere else?'

'Oh, no!' he said quickly, smiling at her out of that
unfailing impulse of contrition – a sort of chivalry. Yet,

walking down the path with her, he blurted out, 'I'd like to go and have a look at those rocks down there.'

She gave the idea her attention. It was a wild-looking place, and there was no one there, but she said, 'Of course, Jerry. When you've had enough, come to the big beach. Or just go straight back to the villa, if you like.' She walked away, that bare arm, now slightly reddened from yesterday's sun, swinging. And he almost ran after her again, feeling it unbearable that she should go by herself, but did not.

She was thinking, Of course he's old enough to be safe without me. Have I been keeping him too close? He mustn't feel he ought to be with me. I must be careful.

He was an only child, eleven years old. She was a widow. She was determined to be neither possessive nor lacking in devotion. She went worrying off to her beach.

As for Jerry, once he saw that his mother had gained her beach, he began the steep descent to the bay. From where he was, high up among red-brown rocks, it was a scoop of moving bluish green fringed with white. As he went lower, he saw that it spread among small promontories and inlets of rough, sharp rock, and the crisping, lapping surface showed stains of purple and darker blue. Finally, as he ran sliding and scraping down the last few yards, he saw an edge of white surf, and the shallow, luminous movement of water over white sand, and, beyond that, a solid, heavy blue.

He ran straight into the water and began swimming. He was a good swimmer. He went out fast over the gleaming sand, over a middle region where rocks lay like discoloured monsters under the surface, and then he was in the real sea—a warm sea where irregular cold currents from the deep water shocked his limbs.

When he was so far out that he could look back not only on the little bay but past the promontory that was between it and the big beach, he floated on the buoyant surface and looked for his mother. There she was, a speck of yellow under an umbrella that looked like a slice of orange peel. He swam back to the shore, relieved at being sure she was there, but all at once very lonely.

On the edge of a small cape that marked the side of the bay away from the promontory was a loose scatter of rocks. Above them, some boys were stripping off their clothes. They came running, naked, down to the rocks. The English boy swam towards them, and kept his distance at a stone's throw. They were of that coast, all of them burned smooth dark brown, and speaking a language he did not understand. To be with them, of them, was a craving that filled his whole body. He swam a little closer; they turned and watched him with narrowed, alert dark eyes. Then one smiled and waved. It was enough. In a minute, he had swum in and was on the rocks beside them, smiling with a desperate, nervous supplication. They shouted cheerful greetings at him, and then, as he preserved his nervous, uncomprehending smile, they understood that he was a foreigner strayed from his own beach, and they proceeded to forget him. But he was happy. He was with them.

They began diving again and again from a high point into a well of blue sea between rough, pointed rocks. After they had dived and come up, they swam around, hauled themselves up, and waited their turn to dive again. They were big boys—men to Jerry. He dived, and they watched him, and when he swam around to take his place, they made way for him. He felt he was accepted, and he dived again, carefully, proud of himself.

Soon the biggest of the boys poised himself, shot down into the water, and did not come up. The others stood about, watching. Jerry, after waiting for the sleek brown head to appear, let out a yell of warning; they looked at him idly and turned their eyes back towards the water. After a long time, the boy came up on the other side of a big dark rock, letting the air out of his lungs in a spluttering gasp and a shout of triumph. Immediately, the rest of them dived in. One moment, the morning seemed full of chattering boys; the next, the air and the surface of the water were empty. But through the heavy blue, dark shapes could be seen moving and groping.

Jerry dived, shot past the school of underwater swimmers, saw a black wall of rock looming at him, touched it, and bobbed up at once to the surface, where the wall was a low barrier he could see across. There was no one visible; under him, in the water, the dim shapes of the swimmers had disappeared. Then one, and then another of the boys came up on the far side of the barrier of rock, and he understood that they had swum through some gap or hole in it. He plunged down again. He could see nothing through the stinging salt water but the blank rock. When he came up the boys were all on the diving rock, preparing to attempt the feat again. And now, in a panic of failure, he yelled up, in English, 'Look at me! Look!' and he

54

began splashing and kicking in the water like a foolish dog.

They looked down gravely, frowning. He knew the frown. At moments of failure, when he clowned to claim his mother's attention, it was with just this grave, embarrassed inspection that she rewarded him. Through his hot shame, feeling the pleading grin on his face like a scar that he could never remove, he looked up at the group of big brown boys on the rock and shouted, *'Bonjour! Merci! Au revoir! Monsieur, monsieur!'* while he hooked his fingers round his ears and waggled them.

Water surged into his mouth; he choked, sank, came up. The rock, lately weighted with boys, seemed to rear up out of the water as their weight was removed. They were flying down past him, now, into the water; the air was full of falling bodies. Then the rock was empty in the hot sunlight. He counted one, two, three. . . .

At fifty, he was terrified. They must all be drowning beneath him, in the watery caves of the rock! At a hundred, he stared around him at the empty hillside, wondering if he should yell for help. He counted faster, faster, to hurry them up, to bring them to the surface quickly, to drown them quickly–anything rather than the terror of counting on and on into the blue emptiness of the morning. And then, at a hundred and sixty, the water beyond the rock was full of boys blowing like brown whales. They swam back to the shore without a look at him.

He climbed back to the diving rock and sat down, feeling the hot roughness of it under his thighs. The boys were gathering up their bits of clothing and

55

running off along the shore to another promontory. They were leaving to get away from him. He cried openly, fists in his eyes. There was no one to see him, and he cried himself out.

It seemed to him that a long time had passed, and he swam out to where he could see his mother. Yes, she was still there, a yellow spot under an orange umbrella. He swam back to the big rock, climbed up, and dived into the blue pool among the fanged and angry boulders. Down he went, until he touched the wall of rock again. But the salt was so painful in his eyes that he could not see.

He came to the surface, swam to shore and went back to the villa to wait for his mother. Soon she walked slowly up the path, swinging her striped bag, the flushed, naked arm dangling beside her. 'I want some swimming goggles,' he panted, defiant and beseeching.

She gave him a patient, inqusitive look as she said casually, 'Well, of course, darling.'

But now, now, now! He must have them this minute, and no other time. He nagged and pestered until she went with him to a shop. As soon as she had bought the goggles, he grabbed them from her hand as if she were going to claim them for herself, and was off, running down the steep path to the bay.

Jerry swam out to the big barrier rock, adjusted the goggles, and dived. The impact of the water broke the rubber-enclosed vacuum, and the goggles came loose. He understood that he must swim down to the base of the rock from the surface of the water. He fixed the goggles tight and firm, filled his lungs, and floated, face down, on the water. Now he could see. It was as if he had eyes of a different kind – fish-eyes that showed everything clear and delicate and wavering in the bright water.

Under him, six or seven feet down, was a floor of perfectly clean, shining white sand, rippled firm and hard by the tides. Two greyish shapes steered there, like long, rounded pieces of wood or slate. They were fish. He saw them nose towards each other, poise motionless, make a dart forward, swerve off, and come around again. It was like a water dance. A few inches above them, the water sparkled as if sequins were dropping through it. Fish again—myriads of minute fish, the length of his fingernail, were drifting through the water, and in a moment he could feel the innumerable tiny touches of them against his limbs. It was like swimming in flaked silver. The great rock the big boys had swum through rose sheer out of the white sand, black, tufted lightly with greenish weed. He could see no gap in it. He swam down to its base.

Again and again he rose, took a big chestful of air, and went down. Again and again he groped over the surface of the rock, feeling it, almost hugging it in the desperate need to find the entrance. And then, once, while he was clinging to the black wall, his knees came up and he shot his feet out forward and they met no obstacle. He had found the hole.

He gained the surface, clambered about the stones that littered the barrier rock until he found a big one, and, with this in his arms, he let himself down over the side of the rock. He dropped, with the weight, straight to the sandy floor. Clinging tight to the anchor of stone, he lay on his side and looked in under the dark shelf at the place where his feet had gone. He could see the hole. It was an irregular, dark gap, but he could not see deep into it. He let go of his anchor, clung with his hands to the edges of the hole, and tried to push himself in.

He got his head in, found his shoulders jammed, moved them in sidewise, and was inside as far as his waist. He could see nothing ahead. Something soft and clammy touched his mouth, he saw a dark frond moving against the greyish rock, and panic filled him. He thought of octopuses, of clinging weed. He pushed himself out backward and caught a glimpse, as he retreated, of a harmless tentacle of seaweed drifting in the mouth of the tunnel. But it was enough. He reached the sunlight, swam to shore, and lay on the diving rock. He looked down into the blue well of water. He knew he must find his way through that cave, or hole, or tunnel, and out the other side.

First, he thought, he must learn to control his breathing. He let himself down into the water with another big stone in his arms, so that he could lie effortlessly on the bottom of the sea. He counted. One, two, three. He counted steadily. He could hear the movement of blood in his chest. Fifty-one, fifty-two. . . . His chest was hurting. He let go of the rock and went up into the air. He saw that the sun was low. He rushed to the villa and found his mother at her supper. She said only 'Did you enjoy yourself?' and he said 'Yes.'

All night, the boy dreamed of the water-filled cave in the rock, and as soon as breakfast was over he went to the bay.

That night, his nose bled badly. For hours he had been underwater, learning to hold his breath, and now he felt weak and dizzy. His mother said, 'I shouldn't overdo things, darling, if I were you.'

That day and the next, Jerry exercised his lungs as if everything, the whole of his life, all that he would become, depended upon it. And again his nose bled at night, and his mother insisted on his coming with her the next day. It was a torment to him to waste a day of his careful self-training, but he stayed with her on that other beach, which now seemed a place for small children, a place where his mother might lie safe in the sun. It was not his beach.

He did not ask for permission, on the following day, to go to his beach. He went, before his mother could consider the complicated rights and wrongs of the matter. A day's rest, he discovered, had improved his count by ten. The big boys had made the passage while he counted a hundred and sixty. He had been counting fast, in his fright. Probably now, if he tried, he could get through that long tunnel, but he was not going to try yet. A curious, most unchildlike persistence, a controlled impatience, made him wait. In the meantime, he lay underwater on the white sand, littered now by stones he had brought down from the upper air, and studied the entrance to the tunnel. He knew every jut and corner of it, as far as it was possible to see. It was as if he already felt its sharpness about his shoulders.

He sat by the clock in the villa, when his mother was not near, and checked his time. He was incredulous and then proud to find he could hold his breath without strain for two minutes. The words 'two minutes', authorised by the clock, brought the adventure that was so necessary to him close.

In another four days, his mother said casually one morning, they must go home. On the day before they left, he would do it. He would do it if it killed him, he said defiantly to himself. But two days before they were to leave—a day of triumph when he increased his count by fifteen—his nose bled so badly that he turned dizzy and had to lie limply over the big rock like a bit of seaweed, watching the thick red blood flow on to the rock and trickle slowly down to the sea. He was frightened. Supposing he turned dizzy in the tunnel? Supposing he died there, trapped? Supposing—his head went around, in the hot sun, and he almost gave up. He thought he would return to the house and lie down, and next summer, perhaps, when he had another year's growth in him—*then* he would go through the hole.

But even after he had made the decision, or thought he had, he found himself sitting up on the rock and looking down into the water, and he knew that now, this moment, when his nose had only just stopped bleeding, when his head was still sore and throbbing—this was the moment when he would try. If he did not do it now, he never would. He was trembling with fear that he would not go, and he was trembling with horror at that long, long tunnel under the rock, under the sea. Even in the open sunlight, the barrier rock seemed very wide and very heavy; tons of rock pressed down on where he would go. If he died there, he would lie until one day—perhaps not before next year—those big boys would swim into it and find it blocked.

He put on his goggles, fitted them tight, tested the vacuum. His hands were shaking. Then he chose the biggest stone he could carry and slipped over the edge of the rock until half of him was in the cool, enclosing water and half in the hot sun. He looked up once at the empty sky, filled his lungs once, twice, and then sank fast to the bottom with the stone. He let it go and began to count. He took the edges of the hole in his hands and drew himself into it, wriggling his shoulders in sidewise as he remembered he must, kicking himself along with his feet.

Soon he was clear inside. He was in a small rock-bound hole filled with yellowish-grey water. The water was pushing him up against the roof. The roof was sharp and pained his back. He pulled himself along with his hands—fast, fast—and used his legs as levers. His head knocked against something; a sharp pain dizzied him. Fifty, fifty-one, fifty-two. . . . He was without light, and the water seemed to press upon him with the weight of rock. Seventy-one, seventy-two. . . . There was no strain on his lungs. He felt like an inflated balloon, his lungs were so light and easy, but his head was pulsing.

He was being continually pressed against the sharp roof, which felt slimy as well as sharp. Again he thought of octopuses, and wondered if the tunnel might be filled with weed that could entangle him. He gave himself a panicky, convulsive kick forward, ducked his head, and swam. His feet and hands moved freely, as if in open water. The hole must have widened out. He thought he must be swimming fast, and he was frightened of banging his head if the tunnel narrowed.

A hundred, a hundred and one. . . . The water paled. Victory filled him. His lungs were beginning to hurt. A few more strokes and he would be out. He was counting wildly; he said a hundred and fifteen, and then, a long time later, a hundred and fifteen again. The water was a clear jewel-green all around him. Then he saw, above his head, a crack running up through the rock. Sunlight was falling through it, showing the clean dark rock of the tunnel, a single mussel shell, and darkness ahead.

He was at the end of what he could do. He looked up at the crack as if it were filled with air and not water, as if he could put his mouth to it to draw in air. A hundred and fifteen, he heard himself say inside his head – but he had said that long ago. He must go on into the blackness ahead, or he would drown. His head was swelling, his lungs cracking. A hundred and fifteen, a hundred and fifteen pounded through his head, and he feebly clutched at rocks in the dark, pulling himself forward, leaving the brief space of sunlight behind. He felt he was dying. He was no longer quite conscious. He struggled on in the darkness between lapses into unconsciousness. An immense, swelling pain filled his head, and then the darkness cracked with an explosion of green light. His hands, groping forward, met nothing, and his feet, kicking back, propelled him out into the open sea.

He drifted to the surface, his face turned up to the air. He was gasping like a fish. He felt he would sink now and drown; he could not swim the few feet back to the rock. Then he was clutching it and pulling himself up on to it. He lay face down, gasping. He could see nothing but a red-veined, clotted dark. His eyes must have burst, he thought; they were full of blood. He tore off his goggles and a gout of blood went into the sea. His nose was bleeding, and the blood had filled the goggles.

He scooped up handfuls of water from the cool, salty sea, to splash on his face, and did not know whether it was blood or salt water he tasted. After a time, his heart quieted, his eyes cleared, and he sat up. He could see the local boys diving and playing half a mile away. He did not want them. He wanted nothing but to get back home and lie down.

In a short while, Jerry swam to shore and climbed slowly up the path to the villa. He flung himself on his bed and slept, waking at the sound of feet on the path outside. His mother was coming back. He rushed to the bathroom, thinking she must not see his face with bloodstains, or tearstains, on it. He came out of the bathroom and met her as she walked into the villa, smiling, her eyes lighting up.

'Have a nice morning?' she asked, laying her hand on his warm brown shoulder a moment.

'Oh, yes, thank you,' he said.

'You look a bit pale.' And then, sharp and anxious, 'How did you bang your head?'

'Oh, just banged it,' he told her.

She looked at him closely. He was strained. His eyes were glazed-looking. She was worried. And then she said to herself, 'Oh, don't fuss! Nothing can happen. He can swim like a fish.'

They sat down to lunch together.

'Mummy,' he said, 'I can stay under water for two minutes – three minutes, at least.' It came bursting out of him.

'Can you, darling?' she said. 'Well, I shouldn't over-do it. I don't think you ought to swim any more today.'

She was ready for a battle of wills, but he gave in at once. It was no longer of the least importance to go to the bay.

63

7

SPIT NOLAN

Bill Naughton

Spit Nolan was a pal of mine. He was a thin lad with a bony face that was always pale, except for two rosy spots on his cheekbones. He had quick brown eyes, short, wiry hair, rather stooped shoulders, and we all knew that he had only one lung. He had a disease which in those days couldn't be cured, unless you went away to Switzerland, which Spit certainly couldn't afford. He wasn't sorry for himself in any way, and in fact we envied him, because he never had to go to school.

Spit was the champion trolley-rider of Cotton Pocket; that was the district in which we lived. He had a very good balance, and sharp wits, and he was very brave, so that these qualities, when added to his skill as a rider, meant that no other boy could ever beat Spit on a trolley–and every lad had one.

Our trolleys were simple vehicles for getting a good ride downhill at a fast speed. To make one you had to get a stout piece of wood about five feet in length and eighteen inches wide. Then you needed four wheels, preferably two pairs, large ones for the back and smaller ones for the front. However, since we bought our wheels from the scrapyard, most trolleys had four odd wheels. Now you had to get a poker and put it in the fire until it was red hot, and then burn a hole through the wood at the front. Usually it would take three or four attempts to get the hole bored through.

Through this hole you fitted the giant nut-and-bolt, which acted as a swivel for the steering. Fastened to the nut was a strip of wood, on to which the front axle was secured by bent nails. A piece of rope tied to each end of the axle served for steering. Then a knob of margarine had to be slanced out of the kitchen to grease the wheels and bearings. Next you had to paint a name on it: *Invincible* or *Dreadnought*, though it might be a motto: *Death before Dishonour* or *Labour and Wait*. That done, you then stuck your chest out, opened the back gate, and wheeled your trolley out to face the critical eyes of the world.

Spit spent most mornings trying out new speed gadgets on his trolley, or searching Enty's scrapyard for good wheels. Afternoons he would go off and have a spin down Cemetery Brew. This was a very steep road that led to the cemetery, and it was very popular with trolley-drivers as it was the only macadamised hill for miles around, all the others being cobblestones for horse traffic. Spit used to lie in wait for a coal-cart or other horse-drawn vehicle, then he would hitch *Egdam* to the back to take it up the brew. *Egdam* was a name in memory of a girl called Madge, whom he had once met at Southport Sanatorium, where he had spent three happy weeks. Only I knew the meaning of it, for he had reversed the letters of her name to keep his love a secret.

It was the custom for lads to gather at the street corner on summer evenings and, trolleys parked at hand, discuss trolleying, road surfaces, and also show off any new gadgets. Then, when Spit gave the sign, we used to set off for Cemetery Brew. There was scarcely any evening traffic on the roads in those days, so that we could have a good practice before our evening race. Split, the unbeaten champion, would inspect every trolley and rider, and allow a start which was reckoned on the size of the wheels and the weight of the rider. He was always the last in the line of starters, though no matter how long a start he gave it seemed impossible to beat him. He knew that road like the palm of his hand, every tiny lump or pothole, and he never came a cropper.

Among us he took things easy, but when occasion asked for it he would go all out. Once he had to meet a challenge from Ducker Smith, the champion of the Engine Row gang. On that occasion Spit borrowed a wheel from the baby's pram, removing one nearest the wall, so it wouldn't be missed, and confident he could replace it before his mother took baby out. And after fixing it to his trolley he made that ride on what was called the 'belly-down' style – that is, he lay full stretch on his stomach, so as to avoid wind resistance. Although Ducker got away with a flying start he had not that sensitive touch of Spit, and his frequent bumps and swerves lost him valuable inches, so that he lost the race with a good three lengths. Spit arrived home just in time to catch his mother as she was wheeling young Georgie off the doorstep, and if he had not made a dash for it the child would have fallen out as the pram overturned.

It happened that we were gathered at the street corner with our trolleys one evening when Ernie Haddock let out a hiccup of wonder: 'Hy, chaps, wot's Leslie got?'

We all turned our eyes on Leslie Duckett, the plump son of the local publican. He approached us on a brand-new trolley, propelled by flicks of his foot on the pavement. From a distance the thing had looked impressive, but now, when it came up among us, we were too dumbfounded to speak. Such a magnificent trolley had never been seen! The riding board was of solid oak, almost two inches thick; four new wheels with pneumatic tyres; a brake, a bell, a lamp, and a spotless steering-cord. In front was a plate on which was the name in bold lettering: *The British Queen*.

'It's called after the pub,' remarked Leslie. He tried to edge it away from Spit's trolley, for it made *Egdam* appear horribly insignificant. Voices had been stilled for a minute, but now they broke out:

'Where'd it come from?'

'How much was it?'

'Who made it?'

Leslie tried to look modest. 'My dad had it specially made to measure,' he said, 'by the gaffer of the Holt Engineering Works.'

He was a nice lad, and now he wasn't sure whether to feel proud or ashamed. The fact was, nobody had ever had a trolley made by somebody else. Trolleys were swopped and so on, but no lad had ever owned one that had been made by other hands. We went quiet now, for Spit had calmly turned his attention to it, and was examining *The British Queen* with his expert eye. First he tilted it, so that one of the rear wheels was off the ground, and after giving it a flick of the finger he listened intently with his ear close to the hub.

'A beautiful ball-bearing race,' he remarked, 'it runs like silk.' Next he turned his attention to the body. 'Grand piece of timber, Leslie – though a trifle on the heavy side. It'll take plenty of pulling up a brew.'

'I can pull it,' said Leslie, stiffening.

'You might find it a shade *front-heavy*,' went on Spit, which means it'll be hard on the steering unless you keep it well oiled.'

'It's well made,' said Leslie. 'Eh, Spit?'

Spit nodded. 'Aye, all the bolts are countersunk,' he said, 'everything chamfered and fluted off to perfection. But—'

'But what?' asked Leslie.

'Do you want me to tell you?' asked Spit.

'Yes, I do,' answered Leslie.

'Well, it's got none of *you* in it,' said Spit.

'How do you mean?' asked Leslie.

'Well, you haven't so much as given it a single tap with a hammer,' said Spit. 'That trolley will be a stranger to you to your dying day.'

'How come,' said Leslie, 'since I *own* it?'

Spit shook his head. 'You don't own it,' he said, in a quiet, solemn tone. 'You own nothing in this world except those things you have taken a hand in the making of, or else you've earned the money to buy them.'

Leslie sat down on *The British Queen* to think this one out. We all sat around, scratching our heads.

'You've forgotten to mention one thing,' said Ernie Haddock to Spit, 'what about the *speed*?'

'Going down a steep hill,' said Spit, 'she should hold the road well—an' with wheels like that she should certainly be able to shift some.'

'Think she could beat *Egdam*?' ventured Ernie.

'That,' said Spit, 'remains to be seen.'

Ernie gave a shout: 'A challenge race! *The British Queen* versus *Egdam*!'

'Not tonight,' said Leslie. 'I haven't got the proper

69

feel of her yet.'

'What about Sunday morning?' I said.

Spit nodded. 'As good a time as any.'

Leslie agreed. 'By then,' he said in a challenging tone, 'I'll be able to handle her.'

Chattering like monkeys, eating bread, carrots, fruit, and bits of toffee, the entire gang of us made our way along the silent Sunday-morning streets for the big race at Cemetery Brew. We were split into two fairly equal sides.

Leslie, in his serge Sunday suit, walked ahead, with Ernie Haddock pulling *The British Queen*, and a bunch of supporters around. They were optimistic, for Leslie had easily outpaced every other trolley during the week, though as yet he had not run against Spit.

Spit was in the middle of the group behind, and I was pulling *Egdam* and keeping the pace easy, for I wanted Spit to keep fresh. He walked in and out among us with an air of imperturbability that, considering the occasion, seemed almost godlike. It inspired a fanatical confidence in us. It was such that Chick Dale, a curly-headed kid with soft skin like a girl's, and a nervous lisp, climbed up on to the spiked railings of the cemetery, and, reaching out with his thin fingers, snatched a yellow rose. He ran in front of Spit and thrust it into a small hole in his jersey.

'I pwesent you with the wose of the winner!' he exclaimed.

'And I've a good mind to present you with a clout on the lug,' replied Spit, 'for pinching a flower from a cemetery. An' what's more, it's bad luck.' Seeing Chick's face, he relented. 'On second thoughts, Chick,

I'll wear it. Ee, wot a 'eavenly smell!'

Happily we went along, and Spit turned to a couple of lads at the back. 'Hy, stop that whistling. Don't forget what day it is – folk want their sleep out.'

A faint sweated glow had come over Spit's face when we reached the top of the hill, but he was as majestically calm as ever. Taking the bottle of cold water from his trolley seat, he put it to his lips and rinsed out his mouth in the manner of a boxer.

The two contestants were called together by Ernie.

'No bumpin' or borin',' he said.

They nodded.

'The winner,' he said, 'is the first who puts the nose of his trolley past the cemetery gates.'

They nodded.

'Now, who,' he asked, 'is to be judge?'

Leslie looked at me. 'I've no objection to Bill,' he said. 'I know he's straight.'

I hadn't realised I was, I thought, but by heck I will be!

'Ernie here,' said Spit, 'can be starter.'

With that Leslie and Spit shook hands.

'Fly down to them gates,' said Ernie to me. He had his father's pigeon-timing watch in his hand. 'I'll be setting 'em off dead on the stroke of ten o'clock.'

I hurried down to the gates. I looked back and saw the supporters lining themselves on either side of the road. Leslie was sitting upright on *The British Queen*. Spit was settling himself to ride belly-down. Ernie Haddock, handkerchief raised in the right hand, eye gazing down on the watch in the left, was counting them off – just like when he tossed one of his father's pigeons.

'Five–four–three–two–one–*Off*!'

Spit was away like a shot. That vigorous toe push sent him clean ahead of Leslie. A volley of shouts went up from his supporters, and groans from Leslie's. I saw Spit move straight to the middle of the road camber. Then I ran ahead to take up my position at the winning-post.

When I turned again I was surprised to see that Spit had not increased the lead. In fact, it seemed that Leslie had begun to gain on him. He had settled himself into a crouched position, and those perfect wheels combined with his extra weight were bringing him up with Spit. Not that it seemed possible he could ever catch him. For Spit, lying flat on his trolley, moving with a fine balance, gliding, as it were, over the rough patches, looked to me as though he were a bird that might suddenly open out its wings and fly clean into the air.

The runners along the side could no longer keep up with the trolleys. And now, as they skimmed past the half-way mark, and came to the very steepest part, there was no doubt that Leslie was gaining. Spit had never ridden better; he coaxed *Egdam* over the tricky parts, swayed with her, gave her head, and guided her. Yet Leslie, clinging grimly to the steering-rope of *The British Queen*, and riding the rougher part of the road, was actually drawing level. Those beautiful ball-bearing wheels, engineer-made, encased in oil, were holding the road, and bringing Leslie along faster than spirit and skill could carry Spit.

Dead level they sped into the final stretch. Spit's slight figure was poised fearlessly on his trolley, drawing the extremes of speed from her. Thundering beside him, anxious but determined, came Leslie. He was actually drawing ahead – and forcing his way to the top of the camber. On they came like two charioteers – Spit delicately edging to the side, to gain inches by the extra downward momentum. I kept my eyes fastened clean across the road as they came belting past the winning-post.

First past was the plate *The British Queen*. I saw that first. Then I saw the heavy rear wheel jog over a pot-hole and strike Spit's front wheel – sending him in a swerve across the road. Suddenly then, from nowhere, a charabanc came speeding round the wide bend.

Spit was straight in its path. Nothing could avoid the collision. I gave a cry of fear as I saw the heavy solid tyre of the front wheel hit the trolley. Spit was flung up and his back hit the radiator. Then the driver stopped dead.

I got there first. Spit was lying on the macadam road on his side. His face was white and dusty, and coming out between his lips and trickling down his chin was a rivulet of fresh red blood. Scattered all about him were yellow rose petals.

'Not my fault,' I heard the driver shouting. 'I didn't have a chance. He came straight at me.'

The next thing we were surrounded by women who had got out of the charabanc. And then Leslie and all the lads came up.

'Somebody send for an ambulance!' called a woman.

'I'll run an' tell the gatekeeper to telephone,' said Ernie Haddock.

'I hadn't a chance,' the driver explained to the women.

'A piece of his jersey on the starting-handle there . . .' said someone.

'Don't move him,' said the driver to a stout woman who had bent over Spit. 'Wait for the ambulance.'

'Hush up,' she said. She knelt and put a silk scarf under Spit's head. Then she wiped his mouth with her little handkerchief.

He opened his eyes. Glazed they were, as though he couldn't see. A short cough came out of him, then he looked at me and his lips moved.

'*Who won?*'

'Thee!' blurted out Leslie. 'Tha just licked me. Eh, Bill?'

'Aye,' I said, 'old *Egdam* just pipped *The British Queen.*'

Spit's eyes closed again. The women looked at each other. They nearly all had tears in their eyes. Then Spit looked up again, and his wise, knowing look came over his face. After a minute he spoke in a sharp whisper:

'Liars. I can remember seeing Leslie's back wheel hit my front 'un. I didn't win – I lost.' He stared upward for a few seconds, then his eyes twitched and shut.

The driver kept repeating how it wasn't his fault, and next thing the ambulance came. Nearly all the women were crying now, and I saw the look that went between the two men who put Spit on a stretcher – but I couldn't believe he was dead. I had to go into the ambulance with the attendant to give him particulars. I went up the step and sat down inside and looked out the little window as the driver slammed the doors. I saw the driver holding Leslie as a witness. Chick Dale was lifting the smashed-up *Egdam* on to the body of

74

The British Queen. People with bunches of flowers in their hands stared after us as we drove off. Then I heard the ambulance man asking me Spit's name. Then he touched me on the elbow with his pencil and said:

'Where *did* he live?'

I knew then. That word 'did' struck right into me. But for a minute I couldn't answer. I had to think hard, for the way he said it made it suddenly seem as though Spit Nolan had been dead and gone for ages.

8

MOTHER AND SON

Liam O'Flaherty .

Although it was only five o'clock, the sun had already set and the evening was very still, as all spring evenings are, just before the birds begin to sing themselves to sleep; or maybe tell one another bedside stories. The village was quiet. The men had gone away to fish for the night after working all the morning with the sowing. Women were away milking the cows in the little fields among the crags.

Brigid Gill was alone in her cottage waiting for her son to come home from school. He was now an hour late, and as he was only nine she was very nervous about him especially as he was her only child and he was a wild boy always getting into mischief, mitching from school, fishing minnows on Sunday and building stone 'castles' in the great crag above the village. She kept telling herself that she would give him a good scolding and beating when he came in, but at the same time her heart was thumping with anxiety and she started at every sound, rushing out to the door and looking down the winding road, that was now dim with the shadows of the evening. So many things could happen to a little boy.

His dinner of dried fish and roast potatoes was being kept warm in the oven among the peat ashes beside the fire on the hearth, and on the table there was a plate, a knife and a little mug full of buttermilk.

At last she heard the glad cries of the schoolboys afar

off, and rushing out she saw them scampering, not up the road, but across the crags to the left, their caps in their hands.

'Thank God,' she said, and then she persuaded herself that she was very angry. Hurriedly she got a small dried willow rod, sat down on a chair within the door and waited for Stephen.

He advanced up the yard very slowly, walking near the stone fence that bounded the vegetable garden, holding his satchel in his left hand by his side, with his cap in his right hand, a red-cheeked slim boy, dressed in close-fitting grey frieze trousers that reached a little below his knees and a blue sweater. His feet were bare and covered with all sorts of mud. His face perspired and his great soft blue eyes were popping out of his head with fright. He knew his mother would be angry.

At last he reached the door and, holding down his head, he entered the kitchen. The mother immediately jumped up and seized him by the shoulder. The boy screamed, dropped his satchel and his cap and clung to her apron. The mother raised the rod to strike, but when she looked down at the trembling body, she began to tremble herself and dropped the stick. Stooping down, she raised him up and began kissing him, crying at the same time with tears in her eyes.

'What's going to become of you at all, at all? God save us, I haven't the courage to beat you and you're breaking my heart with your wickedness.'

The boy sobbed, hiding his head in his mother's bosom.

'Go away,' she said, thrusting him away from her, 'and eat your dinner. Your father will give to you a good thrashing in the morning. I've spared you often

77

and begged him not to beat you, but this time I'm not going to say a word for you. You've my heart broken, so you have. Come here and eat your dinner.'

She put the dinner on the plate and pushed the boy into the chair. He sat down sobbing, but presently he wiped his eyes with his sleeve and began to eat ravenously. Gradually his face brightened and he moved about on the chair, settling himself more comfortably and forgetting all his fears of his mother and the thrashing he was going to get next morning in the joy of satisfying his hunger. The mother sat on the doorstep, knitting in silence and watching him lovingly from under her long black eyelashes.

All her anger had vanished by now and she felt glad that she had thrust all the responsibility for punishment on to her husband. Still, she wanted to be severe, and although she wanted to ask Stephen what he had been doing, she tried to hold her tongue. At last, however, she had to talk.

'What kept you, Stephen?' she said softly.

Stephen swallowed the last mouthful and turned around with his mug in his hand.

'We were only playing ball,' he said excitedly, 'and then Red Michael ran after us and chased us out of his field where we were playing. And we had to run an awful way; oh, a long, long way we had to run, over crags where I never was before.'

'But didn't I often tell you not to go into people's fields to play ball?'

'Oh, mother, sure it wasn't me but the other boys that wanted to go, and if I didn't go with them they'd say I was afraid, and father says I mustn't be afraid.'

'Yes, you pay heed to your father but you pay no

78

Mother and Son

heed to your mother that has all the trouble with you. Now and what would I do if you fell running over the crags and sprained your ankle?'

And she put her apron to her eyes to wipe away a tear.

Stephen left his chair, came over to her and put his arms around her neck.

'Mother,' he said, 'I'll tell you what I saw on the crags if you promise not to tell father about me being late and playing ball in Red Michael's field.'

'I'll do no such thing,' she said.

'Oh, do, mother,' he said, 'and I'll never be late again, never, never, never.'

'All right, Stephen; what did you see, my little treasure?'

He sat down beside her on the threshold and, looking wistfully out into the sky, his eyes became big and dreamy and his face assumed an expression of mystery and wonder.

'I saw a great big black horse,' he said, 'running in the sky over our heads, but none of the other boys saw it but me, and I didn't tell them about it. The horse had seven tails and three heads and its belly was so big you could put our house into it. I saw it with my two eyes. I did, mother. And then it soared and galloped away, away, ever so far. Isn't that a great thing I saw, mother?'

'It is, darling,' she said dreamily, looking out into the sky, thinking of something with soft eyes. There was silence. Then Stephen spoke again without looking at her.

'Sure you won't tell on me, mother?'

'No, treasure, I won't.'

'On your soul you won't?'

'Hush! little one. Listen to the birds. They are beginning to sing. I won't tell at all. Listen to the beautiful ones.'

They both sat in silence, listening and dreaming, both of them.

9

THE LOST POUND NOTE *

Raymond Williams

As Harry rode back through the village, he passed Will
on his way to school. He was in a group of children,
walking together up the narrow road. There were the
Jenkins children, Gwyn, Glynis, and Beth, from the
cottage next to the Lippys; Howard Watkins, Will's
age, from the chapel cottage; and little Cemlyn Powell,
son of the widowed schoolmistress who lived next door
to the Hybarts. Cemlyn was better dressed than the
other children, but smaller for his age, and pale. Will
walked in the middle of the group, carrying a stick. He
was proud to be walking beside the leader of the group,
a big boy of thirteen, who was already the size of a man.
This was Elwyn Davey, from the poor family, the
Daveys, whose earth-floored cottage by the Honddu
had been flooded several times this past winter. Elwyn
was exceptionally strong and resourceful, the acknow-
ledged master of the school in the playground, and a
match, if it came to it, for William Evans the school-
master himself, who simply waited resignedly for this
impossible boy to leave. On Will's first day at school,
Elwyn had taken him under his protection, warning
the other boys off him and teaching him how to start to
wrestle. Often, on the way home, he carried Will on his
back, taking him down sometimes to the river, where
he would wade in among the stones, with Will on his

---

*A chapter from *Border Country*, a long novel.

back, or sometimes, leaving Will on the sand near the acrid 'wild rhubarb'· leaves, wade out himself into a deeper pool, and bend to tickle for trout. Whenever he could Elwyn took off his boots and went barefoot, though in the winters at least there was always an old pair of boots that more or less fitted him. Often he would carry Will home and put him down inthe porch, breathless and laughing. Ellen did not like him, and asked Harry to tell him not to take Will off to the river. But Harry did nothing; he thought Elwyn was a fine boy.

'Hurry up, you young shavers, you'll be late,' he called as he rode past.

'Ain't shaving quite yet, Mr Price,' Elwyn shouted back, laughing.

Harry's regular term for the children was gradually being attached to Will: in school now, most of the boys called him 'Shaver'. But Elwyn always called him Will, and offered to stop the nickname if the little boy wanted it.

'No, I got lots of names,' Will said to him. 'My real name's Matthew Henry. It's on my birthday paper. Honest, I saw it. Dada showed me.'

'Making out you can read,' Elwyn laughed.

'I can too. Dada showed me how before I came to school.'

'Reading,' Elwyn said, and laughed as if it were the greatest joke in the world.

'It's all right. What's wrong with it?'

Elwyn looked down at him, and put his hand across his shoulders. 'You like what you want to, Will. Don't let them stop you.'

Will smiled, showing his missing front teeth. 'And

we've got a book,' he said, 'called *English Authors*. We read to each other out of it.'

'Aye, English,' Elwyn said. 'Only here we're Welsh.'

'We talk English, Elwyn.'

'That's different.'

'How's it different?'

Elwyn hesitated, and then laughed. 'Come on now,' he said, 'race you to the gate, give you half-way start.'

'Aye.'

Farther down the road, some way behind the children, Harry passed Mrs Powell, small and thin-faced, her head down as she hurried.

'Morning then.'

'Oh, yes, good morning, Mr Price. Not working?'

'No. All out today.'

'You'd say something if we sent your kids home, not teaching them.'

'That's different,' Harry called back, and rode on. The answer came easily, but for much of the morning he went on thinking of what she had said.

As for money, the strike could not have come at a worse time. He had been saving regularly, but only a few weeks before had spent all his reserve, and a bit from his wages, on a new honey extractor and a season's supply of jars. By autumn, these would show a profit, but there, now, was the money locked up. There would, of course, be the strike pay – twenty-four shillings a week. But while for a week or so this might be enough, it would mean postponing payments and even getting into debt, which he could not face. Ellen had not complained about the strike, but she doubted whether she could manage on the twenty-four shillings, and he knew that he must get what other money he could. In the gardens there were ten dozen sweet-william plants, and about eight dozen hearted lettuce, that he could take to market to sell. Later, though it was the wrong time, he might sell some of the hens. Meanwhile, and likely to be easiest, he might get in advance his May wages as groundsman at the bowling-green – a part-time job he had started in the autumn, when the old groundsman had died.

The rent was due on the following Monday, and since he now paid monthly, he planned to take a pound from the strike-pay and replace it with the pound he hoped to get from the bowls club. But he did not want to ask for this at once. He had drawn his April money only a few days before, at the end of the month, and William Evans had made so much of a formality of it that Harry did not want to go back again so soon. He decided to go on the Saturday, when he had prepared the green for the usual Saturday afternoon game. But in case he did not get it, he put the pound from the strike pay aside at once – in the usual place behind the caddy in the back-kitchen.

On the Friday the old couple next door, the Lewises, asked Will to go to the shop. They had got into the habit of asking this errand, and Will was always keen, for he got a penny for sweets out of the change. That Friday, as he came home from school, Mrs Lewis called him and Will went in to tell his mother.

'Go on then,' she said, 'get it done before your tea.'

Harry was up with Edwin on the farm, and tea might be as late as six or half-past.

'Anything you want, Mam?'

'No, boy, no. Got to go easy now with the strike.'

Will ran off, and into the Lewises. Ellen saw him

come out soon after, carrying a frail and a long leather purse. Then she could only see his hair above the hedge as he walked away down the lane. She was making a dress, sitting in the back-kitchen with the door open on the warm, quiet evening. As she went on working she did not notice the time, and though once or twice she thought that Will should be back, she was not worried till Harry arrived. Looking up at the alarm clock, she saw that it was past six.

'You didn't see Will down the lane?'

'No. What's he, playing?'

'The Lewises sent him down the shop. He ought to be back long ago. I just didn't think the time.'

Harry put down the bag of greens he was carrying. His forehead was covered with sweat, and his clothes were dirty and heavy on his body.

'He'll be all right.'

'He's gone to play, I expect, with that Elwyn,' Ellen said.

'Elwyn'll look after him.'

'Well, it's late. I want him back.'

He stood for a few moments, and then went out to his bike. 'I'll run down and get him then. Got tea ready?'

'Aye, soon as you're back.'

Harry free-wheeled down the lane, letting the stiffness go from his legs. At the road he turned right, and rode slowly, looking around. He reached the shop without seeing any sign of Will.

The shop was a room in an ordinary house. It was run by a widow, Mrs Preece, who had served in the old shop next the chapel, before old Mrs Jenkins died. Preece had been a platelayer, and had been killed on the line.

Harry put his bike against the wall, and went up the steps and through the door, on which the big spring bell jangled. The usual smell of the shop greeted him: leather, bacon, cheese, sweets, oil, fresh bread. Mrs Preece came from the back room, through the tasselled green curtain. At thirty she was still the exceptionally beautiful girl Harry remembered from the few months of her marriage.

'Oh, Mr Price, come after Will?'

'Yes. He been here?'

'He came, now just after four. For some things for the Lewises. Only he'd lost the money.'

'How much?'

'Well, a pound. Of course I'd have let him have the things, I said take them. Only he was upset you know. I told him go back and tell his Mam.'

'He hasn't come. A pound, did you say?'

'It was too much to give him, wasn't it? I thought that. Only he come in, see, with the purse, like he always does, put it on the counter. I got the things, and then picked the purse up and opened it. There wasn't nothing in it but a hairpin, only he said there must be, Mrs Lewis had said there was a pound note.'

Harry listened, staring past her, feeling the sweat across his forehead and the tightness of his chest.

'I must find him,' he said. 'Thank you.'

He ran back to the road, and crossed over to a glat in the hedge. The Daveys' cottage was at the bottom of the field. He hurried down, calling for Will.

'Here.'

He looked round, but could see nobody. Then Elwyn appeared, crawling from the foot of a holly bush.

'He's here, he's all right.'

'Bring him out.'

Elwyn helped Will out through the narrow passage from their hide under the holly bush. His bright hair was dishevelled as he looked up and avoided his father's eyes.

'You lost that money. Why didn't you come home and say?'

Will did not answer. Harry could see that he was nearly crying.

'Money,' said Elwyn. 'What money you lost now, Will? Come on.'

Again Will said nothing. As Elwyn put his hand on his shoulder, he turned his face and rubbed it against Elwyn's sleeve.

'The Lewises give him a pound to go to the shop. When he got there, he'd lost it.'

'A pound?' Elwyn said, his eyes widening. 'No, Will, why didn't you tell me? If he'd told me, Mr Price, I'd have brought him straight back. I'd have looked for it, Will. We'd have found it.'

'That's what we better do now.'

'Aye. Come on, Will. No use being a baby.'

'I didn't lose it,' Will said. 'I couldn't have. I didn't open the purse.'

'How d'you know it was there then?' Elwyn asked sharply.

'Mrs Lewis said. I saw her get it down from the mantel.'

'Then you must have opened it,' Elwyn said impatiently. 'Or it'd be there in the shop.'

'There was only an old pin, hairpin Mrs Preece

said,' Will insisted, and at last looked up at his father.

'We'll look,' Harry said. 'Come on.'

'Where's the purse now?' Elwyn asked, as they walked to the road.

'I hid it, Elwyn. Inside the frail.'

'Where?'

'Them nettles by the hedge.'

'Will boy, you're daft. Come on, show me.'

The boys ran ahead, and at once recovered the frail. Elwyn felt inside for the purse, and opened it.

'That's right. Only a hairpin.'

Harry climbed the hedge in front of the boys, and jumped down into the road. Elwyn, turning, helped Will over, and they ran to catch up. Harry went back to the door of the shop and looked carefully along the path and back down the steps.

'Which side the road did you walk, boy?'

'This side, Dada.'

'All the way?'

'Yes.'

Elwyn looked suspiciously down at Will. 'You didn't go off anywhere else now, Will? No fibs now mind.'

'I walked straight down here, Elwyn. Honest.'

'You sure?'

'I'm sure. And I didn't open the purse either.'

'You must have.'

Harry had gone ahead, walking along the side of the road, looking down in the camber, and along the scythed grass bank.

'Come on, you two.'

The boys followed. Elwyn looked carefully along the bank as he walked. Will did not look, but walked head down. They reached the lane, but found nothing.

89

Elwyn had collected three old Woodbine packets, and several other dirty scraps of paper. Harry barely looked at them. In the lane, he again asked where Will had walked, and brought him up beside him to show. They made their way slowly up the lane, with Elwyn busily searching some yards behind. But nothing had been found when they reached the houses. Ellen was out standing with old Mrs Lewis at the Lewises' gate.

'You found him then?'

'Aye, found him, only he's lost the money.'

'Lost the pound note,' Mrs Lewis cried. 'Oh, Will, you never.'

'I didn't lose it,' Will said, looking straight up at his mother. 'When I took out the purse in the shop there was nothing in it. Only an old pin.'

'But there must have been, Will. I put it in myself. I remember folding it.

'You must have opened the purse and dropped it,' Ellen said.

'We've looked all the way,' Harry said impatiently. Then he turned back and looked at Ellen. She met his eyes, and he saw her suddenly as very young still, almost a child herself, with a child's expression of helplessness and fright.

'You shouldn't have given a child so much,' Harry said roughly, to Mrs Lewis.

'Wait, Harry,' Ellen pleaded.

'I know, Mr Price, only there wasn't the change,' Mrs Lewis said anxiously. 'It's all the money we got in the house see.'

Harry looked round, letting his eyes fall on Elwyn. It was only with Elwyn, now, that he could feel any contact.

'Still, since you give it him and he took it, I'm responsible. I'll pay you the pound.'

'Harry, wait,' Ellen said.

'And I got to go back down for my bike. What was it
you wanted?'

Mrs Lewis looked up at him with tears on the edge of
her eyes. She pushed her fingers back over her thin
hair, unable to speak. Will, meanwhile, had moved a
little away and was stroking the head of the old collie.

'I'll fetch your bike, Mr Price,' Elwyn offered.

'No. Now, what was it, Mrs Lewis? Don't make it
worse now.'

'Half a pound of tea it was, two boxes of matches,
and a half a pint of vinegar, the bottle's in the frail.'

'Right,' Harry said, and walked on to his own gate.
Ellen turned and followed him.

'Will,' Harry called back, 'come on in with your
Mam.'

Will left the dog and followed. Harry went into the
back-kitchen and took the pound from behind the
caddy. He came out and met Ellen and Will on the
path.

'Will, go on in,' Ellen said, and the child obeyed.
'But Harry,' she said urgently, 'you're not giving her
the pound back. Not now?'

'The change from it.'

'I don't know what you think we're going to manage
on.'

'That can wait. I'll see to it.'

'I tell you,' Ellen said, and lowered her voice. 'You
don't think Elwyn got it off him? You know what that
family's like?'

'I know they're poor.'

'Well, then?'

'So are we poor, and Elwyn's a decent boy.'

He went past her and out into the lane. Mrs Lewis had gone back into the house, but Elwyn was waiting, holding the frail. Harry took it, and Elwyn walked beside him down the lane. For a long way down they did not speak, but then Elwyn said suddenly: 'You believe me, Mr Price, don't you? If I'd have known, I'd have brought him straight up. I thought his Mam knew, see, he was out to play.'

'It's not your fault. Don't think about it,' Harry said. He was walking fast, still watching the ground. They did not speak again until they reached the shop. Harry went straight in, and the bell jangled again. He realised that he had pushed too hard at the door.

'Found it then, Mr Price?'

'No. It's gone.'

'It's a shame now. A pound!'

Harry looked at her, and was at once strangely relaxed. She must have felt his look, for she flushed slightly, and put her hand nervously to her hair.

'I've come for the stuff anyhow.'

'It's all here ready, Mr Price.'

'Give us the change from that,' he said, and put down the note he had been holding.

'You paying it yourself then?'

'This the lot?' Harry said, packing the things into the frail. 'What about the vinegar?'

'Oh, yes, I didn't take the bottle, did I?'

He passed the bottle across, and Mrs Preece filled it from a stone jar, behind a hanging rack of dresses, aprons, and coats. 'Right,' she said, wiping the bottle on her apron, and putting it on the counter. She took the note, and counted the change. Harry put the change in his pocket, without counting it.

'Good night, thank you,' he said, and went out.

Elwyn was waiting for him at the foot of the steps, holding the bike.

He took it and stepped over the saddle. He rode back quickly, and at the pitch in the lane, where he usually dismounted and walked, he stood on his pedals and rode, glad to feel his strength. He was breathing hard when he reached the houses, and the sweat had run down into his eyes. The first thing he saw was Ellen running out to him, laughing.

'It's found,' he heard her shout, and as he heard the words his strength seemed to ebb. He drew back and got off the bike.

'Found?'

'She never put it in. She took it down ready, and left it on the table.'

Harry seemed not to be listening. He stared down through the frame of the bike, then: 'Catch!' he said suddenly, and threw the frail across. Ellen, surprised, nearly dropped it.

'And here's the change,' he said, grabbing the money from his pocket. 'Bring back the pound.'

She watched him, surprised. She had expected pleasure, or at least relief. This hard edge of withdrawal and anger was frightening. He walked on without speaking, and put his bike away under the porch. He went into the back-kitchen, which was now almost dark. Will was sitting on a chair between the table and the copper; far back against the wall, his feet not reaching the ground. Harry went to him and bent down.

'You know it's found, Will?'

'Mam said she didn't put it in.'

'I'm sorry. Honestly, I'm sorry,' Harry said, and bent forward so that his head touched the boy's shoulder.

'Not for you to be sorry, Dada,' Will said, but pushed the head away.

Ellen came in behind them, quietly.

'I got the pound, Harry. And the twopence she made me bring, for Will's sweets.'

'I don't want her old twopence,' Will shouted.

'Leave it all,' Harry said, sharply, and got up. 'I'll hear no more about it. Now get the lamp lit, and we'll have some food.'

Ellen, suddenly quiet, obeyed.

10

ONE OF THE VIRTUES

Stan Barstow

The watch belonged to my grandfather and it hung on
a hook by the head of his bed where he had lain for
many long weeks. The face was marked off in Roman
numerals, the most elegant figures I had ever seen. The
case was of gold, heavy and beautifully chased; and
the chain was of gold too, and wonderfully rich and
smooth in the hand. The mechanism, when you held
the watch to your ear, gave such a deep, steady ticking
that you could not imagine its ever going wrong. It was
altogether a most magnificent watch and when I sat
with my grandfather in the late afternoon, after school,
I could not keep my eyes away from it, dreaming that
someday I too might own such a watch.

It was almost a ritual for me to sit with my grandfather for a little while after tea. My mother said he was
old and drawing near his time, and it seemed to me
that he must be an incredible age. He liked me to read
to him from the evening paper while he lay there, his
long hands, soft and white now from disuse and fined
down to skin and bone by illness and age, fluttered
restlessly about over the sheets, like a blind man reading braille. He had never been much of a reader himself and it was too much of an effort for him now.
Possibly because he had had so little education, no one
believed in it more, and he was always eager for news
of my progress at school. The day I brought home the
news of my success in the County Minor Scholarship

examination he sent out for half an ounce of twist and found the strength to sit up in bed for a smoke.

'Grammar School next, then, Will?' he said, pleased as Punch.

'Then college,' I said, seeing the path straight before me. 'Then I shall be a doctor.'

'Aye, that he will, I've no doubt,' my grandfather said. 'But he'll need plenty o' patience afore that day. Patience an' hard work, Will lad.'

Though as I have said, he had little book-learning, I thought sometimes as I sat with my grandfather that he must be one of the wisest men in Yorkshire; and these two qualities—patience and the ability to work hard—were the cornerstones of his philosophy of life.

'Yes, Grandad,' I told him. 'I can wait.'

'Aye, Will, that's t'way to do it. That's t'way to get on, lad.'

The smoke was irritating his throat and he laid aside the pipe with a sigh that seemed to me to contain regret for all the bygone pleasures of a lifetime and he fidgeted with the sheets. 'It must be gettin' on, Will . . .'

I took down the watch and gave it to him. He gazed at it for some moments, winding it up a few turns. When he passed it back to me I held it, feeling the weight of it.

'I reckon he'll be after a watch like that hisself, one day, eh, Will?'

I smiled shyly, for I had not meant to covet the watch so openly. 'Someday, Grandad,' I said. I could never *really* imagine the day such a watch could be mine.

'That watch wa' gi'n me for fifty year o' service wi' my firm,' my grandfather said. ' "A token of appreciation," they said . . . It's theer, in t'back, for you to see . . .'

I opened the back and looked at the inscription there: 'For loyal service . . .'

Fifty years . . . My grandfather had been a black-smith. It was hard now to believe that those pale, almost transparent hands had held the giant tongs or directed the hammer in its mighty downward swing. Fifty years . . . Five times my own age. And the watch, prize of hard work and loyalty, hung, proudly cherished, at the head of the bed in which he was resting out his days. I think my grandfather spoke to me as he did partly because of the great difference in our ages and partly because of my father. My mother never spoke of my father and it was my grandfather who cut away some of the mystery with which my mother's silence had shrouded him. My father, Grandfather told me, had been a promising young man cursed with a weakness. Impatience was his weakness: he was impatient to make money, to be a success, to impress his friends; and he lacked the perseverance to approach success steadily. One after the other he abandoned his projects, and he and my mother were often unsure of their next meal. Then at last, while I was still learning to walk, my father, reviling the lack of opportunity in the mother country, set off for the other side of the world and was never heard of again. All this my grandfather told me not with bitterness or anger, for I gathered he had liked my father, but with sorrow that a good man should have gone astray for want of what, to my grandfather, was a simple virtue, and brought such a hard life to my mother, Grand-father's daughter.

So my grandfather drifted to the end; and remembering those restless fingers I believe he came as near to losing his patience then as at any time in his long life.

One evening at the height of summer, as I prepared to leave him for the night, he put out his hand and touched mine. 'Thank y', lad,' he said in a voice grown very tired and weak. 'An' he'll not forget what I've told him?'

I was suddenly very moved; a lump came into my throat. 'No, Grandad,' I told him, 'I'll not forget.'

He gently patted my hand, then looked away and closed his eyes. The next morning my mother told me that he had died in his sleep.

They laid him out in the damp mustiness of his own front room, among the tasselled chairback covers and the lustres under their thin glass domes; and they let me see him for a moment. I did not stay long with him. He looked little different from the scores of times I had seen him during his illness, except that his fretting hands were stilled beneath the sheet and his hair and moustache had the inhuman antiseptic cleanliness of death. Afterwards, in the quiet of my own room, I cried a little, remembering that I should see him no more, and that I had talked with him and read to him for the last time.

After the funeral the family descended upon us in force for the reading of the will. There was not much to quarrel about: my grandfather had never made much money, and what little he left had been saved slowly, thriftily over the years. It was divided fairly evenly along with the value of the house, the only condition being that the house was not to be sold, but that my mother was to be allowed to live in it and take part of her livelihood from Grandfather's smallholding (which she had in fact managed during his illness) for as long as she liked, or until she married again, which was not likely, since no one knew whether my father was alive or dead.

It was when they reached the personal effects that we got a surprise, for my grandfather had left his watch to me!

'Why your Will?' my Uncle Henry asked in surly tones. 'I've two lads o' me own and both older than Will.'

'An' neither of 'em ever seemed to know their grandfather was poorly,' my mother retorted, sharp as a knife.

'Young an' old don't mix,' Uncle Henry muttered, and my mother, thoroughly ruffled, snapped back, 'Well, Will an' his grandfather mixed very nicely, and your father was right glad of his company when there wasn't so much of anybody else's.'

This shot got home on Uncle Henry, who had been a poor sick-visitor. It never took my family long to work up a row and listening from the kitchen through the partly open door, I waited for some real north-country family sparring. But my Uncle John, Grandfather's eldest son, and a fair man, chipped in and put a stop to it. 'Now that's enough,' he rumbled in his deep voice. 'We'll have no wranglin' wi' the old man hardly in his coffin.' There was a short pause and I could imagine him looking round at everyone. 'I'd a fancy for that watch meself, but me father knew what he was about an' if he chose to leave it to young Will, then I'm not goin' to argue about it.' And that was the end of it; the watch was mine.

The house seemed very strange without my grandfather and during the half-hour after tea, when it had
been my custom to sit with him, I felt for a long time
greatly at a loss. The watch had a lot to do with this
feeling. I still admired it in the late afternoon but now
it hung by the mantelshelf in the kitchen where I had
persuaded my mother to let it be. My grandfather and
his watch had always been inseparable in my mind,
and to see the watch without at the same time seeing
him was to feel keenly the awful finality of his going.
The new position of the watch was in the nature of a
compromise between my mother and me. While it was
officially mine, it was being held in trust by my mother
until she considered me old enough and careful enough
to look after it. She was all for putting it away till that
time, but I protested so strongly that she finally agreed
to keep it in the kitchen where I could see it all the
time, taking care, however, to have it away in a
drawer when any of the family were expected, because,
she said, there was no point in 'rubbing it in'.

The holiday came to an end and it was time for me
to start my first term at the Grammar School in
Cressley. A host of new excitements came to fill my
days. I was cast into the melting pot of the first form
and I had to work for my position in that new fraternity
along with twenty-odd other boys from all parts of the
town. Friendships were made in those first weeks
which would last into adult life. One formed first
opinions about one's fellows, and one had one's own
label stuck on according to the first impression made.
For first impressions seemed vital, and it looked as
though the boy who was lucky or clever enough to
assert himself favourably at the start would have an

advantage for the rest of his schooldays.

There are many ways in which a boy—or a man—may try to establish himself with his fellows. One or two of my classmates grovelled at everyone's feet, while others took the opposite line and tried systematically to beat the form into submission, starting with the smallest boy and working up till they met their match. Others charmed everyone by their skill at sports, and others by simply being themselves and seeming hardly to make any effort at all. I have never made friends easily and I was soon branded as aloof. For a time I did little more than get on speaking terms with my fellows.

One of our number was the youngest son of a well-to-do local tradesman and he had a brother who was a prefect in the sixth. His way of asserting himself was to parade his possessions before our envious eyes; and while these tactics did not win him popularity they gained him a certain following and made him one of the most discussed members of the form. Crawley's bicycle was brand new and had a three-speed gear, an oil-bath gearcase, a speedometer, and other desirable refinements. Crawley's fountain pen matched his propelling pencil and had a gold nib. His football boots were of the best hide and his gym slippers were reinforced with rubber across the toes. Everything, in fact, that Crawley had was better than ours. Until he brought the watch.

He flashed it on his wrist with arrogant pride, making a great show of looking at the time. His eldest brother had brought it from abroad. He'd even smuggled it through the customs especially for him. Oh, yes, said Crawley, it had a sweep second-hand and luminous figures, and wasn't it absolutely the finest watch we had ever seen? But I was thinking of my grandfather's watch: *my* watch now. There had never been a watch to compare with that. With heart-thumping excitement I found myself cutting in on Crawley's self-satisfied eulogy.

'I've seen a better watch than that.'

'Gerraway!'

'Yes I have,' I insisted. 'It was my grandfather's. He left it to me when he died.'

'Well show us it,' Crawley said.

'I haven't got it here.'

'You haven't got it at all,' Crawley said. 'You can't show us it to prove it.'

I could have knocked the sneer from his hateful face in rage that he could doubt the worth of the watch for which my grandfather had worked fifty years.

'I'll bring it this afternoon,' I said; 'then you'll see!'

The hand of friendship was extended tentatively in my direction several times that morning. I should not be alone in my pleasure at seeing Crawley taken down a peg. As the clock moved with maddening slowness to half-past twelve I thought with grim glee of how in one move I would settle Crawley's boasting and assert myself with my fellows. On the bus going home, however, I began to wonder how on earth I was going to persuade my mother to let me take the watch out of doors. But I had forgotten that today was Monday, washing day, when my mother put my grandfather's watch in a drawer, away from the steam. I had only to wait for her to step outside for a moment and I could slip the watch into my pocket. She would not miss it before I came home for tea. And if she did, it would be too late.

I was too eager and excited to wait for the return bus and after dinner I got my bike out of the shed. My mother watched me from the kitchen doorway and I could imagine her keen eyes piercing the cloth of my blazer to where the watch rested guiltily in my pocket.

'Are you going on your bike, then, Will?'

I said, 'Yes, Mother,' and, feeling uncomfortable under that direct gaze, began to wheel the bike across the yard.

'I thought you said it needed mending or something before you rode it again . . .?'

'It's only a little thing,' I told her. 'It'll be all right.'

I waved good-bye and pedalled out into the street while she watched me, a little doubtfully, I thought. Once out of sight of the house I put all my strength on the pedals and rode like the wind. My grandfather's house was in one of the older parts of the town and my way led through a maze of steep cobbled streets between long rows of houses. I kept up my speed, excitement coursing through me as I thought of the watch and revelled in my hatred of Crawley. Then from an entry between two terraces of houses a mongrel puppy darted into the street. I pulled at my back brake. The cable snapped with a click – that was what I had intended to fix. I jammed on the front brake with the puppy cowering foolishly in my path. The bike jarred to a standstill, the back end swinging as though cata-pulted over the pivot of the stationary front wheel, and I went over the handlebars.

A man picked me up out of the gutter. 'All right, lad?'

I nodded uncertainly. I seemed unhurt. I rubbed my knees and the side on which I had fallen. I felt the

outline of the watch. Sick apprehension overcame me, but I waited till I was round the next corner before dismounting again and putting a trembling hand into my pocket. Then I looked down at what was left of my grandfather's proudest possession. There was a deep bulge in the back of the case. The glass was shattered and the Roman numerals looked crazily at one another across the pierced and distorted face. I put the watch back in my pocket and rode slowly on, my mind numb with misery.

I thought of showing them what was left; but that was no use. I had promised them a prince among watches and no amount of beautiful wreckage would do.

'Where's the watch, Will?' they asked. 'Have you brought the watch?'

'My mother wouldn't let me bring it,' I lied, moving to my desk, my hand in my pocket clutching the shattered watch.

'His mother wouldn't let him,' Crawley jeered. 'What a tale!'

(Later, Crawley, I thought. The day will come.)

The others took up his cries. I was branded as a romancer, a fanciful liar. I couldn't blame them after letting them down.

The bell rang for first class and I sat quietly at my desk, waiting for the master to arrive. I opened my books and stared blindly at them as a strange feeling stole over me. It was not the mocking of my classmates –they would tire of that eventually. Nor was it the thought of my mother's anger, terrible though that would be. No, all I could think of–all that possessed my mind–was the old man, my grandfather–lying in his bed after a long life of toil, his hands fretting with the sheets, and his tired breathy voice saying, 'Patience, Will, patience.'

And I nearly wept, for it was the saddest moment of my young life.